To Line

MW00461354

WINTER WISHES

TARA GRACE ERICSON

Turn your wishes into prayers and watch God work!

Tara Grace Ericson

SILVER FOUNTAIN PRESS

Paperback ISBN-13: 978-1-949896-02-2
Ebook ISBN:-13: 978-1-949896-03-9

CONTENTS

To my lovely friend, Gabriel.
Our first adventure together was to a library - and I
knew even then (now more than 15 years ago!) I'd
found a kindred spirit in yours. Life is incredibly
different than it was back then, but the blessing of our
constant friendship means more to me than you know.

I will turn the darkness into light before them and make the rough places smooth. These are the things I will do, I will not forsake them.

— *Isaiah 42:9b*

*C*hristine Mathes stared blankly at her mother, not fully understanding what was being said. *Did she just say Florida?* She sat across from her parents in the small eat-in kitchen of her childhood home. The surroundings; the oak table, the worn placemats, and thin off-white Corian plates; were comfortingly familiar. In stark contrast to the familiar setting was the discussion she was having with her parents.

"You're going to Florida?" She wasn't sure if that was the second or third time she had asked the question.

"Not just going, sweetie. We are moving to Florida. Our friends, Russell and Susan—you remember them, don't you? They have a condo there and they say it is just wonderful. We are so tired of Indiana winters, all that snow and ice. You understand, right?"

Chrissy struggled to catch up. "You're moving. To Florida. In a month?"

Her parents shared a glance and her mother spoke again. "Well, we'd like to move down there before Christmas, before the weather gets worse. We've been talking with a realtor down there and he thinks we should have no problem finding something that we can move into right away."

"It just seems so sudden." Chrissy tried to catch up, to slow down the conversation. Wasn't this something her parents should have talked to her about before?

It was then that her father interjected. "You are going to do a great job, Chrissy. We just know it."

Great job? Chrissy started to think of all the implications of this sudden move. "A great job doing what?" She was afraid she knew the answer to this question. She'd occasionally wondered what would happen if her parents ever decided to retire. Until now, though, she pretty much thought they never would. They'd never so much as hinted at leaving Minden. The café was their life. They'd purchased the place nearly thirty-five years ago and had both worked cooking and managing it all these years since. What was Bud and Janine's cafe without Bud and Janine?

"Why, running the café, of course. You are a great waitress and everyone loves you. Besides, the café has to stay in the family! We couldn't bear the thought of selling it. We've been saving our nickels outside of the business for years, and we can afford to move to Florida while you take over as owner of Bud and Janine's. Isn't that great?" Her mother clapped as she delivered the last line with an expectant smile on her face, as though there was no other possible reaction for Chrissy to have than to be over the moon at her good fortune.

Chrissy stirred the mashed potatoes around on her plate, no longer able to take another bite. She thought she might need another glass of wine, though. She attempted a smile, "Yeah, that's amazing, Mom. Both of you, I'm really happy for you." Chrissy was happy for her parents. She was glad they were doing something they'd always wanted to do. Apparently. But the café? She didn't know a thing about running a café. Chrissy was a waitress, sometimes a fill-in cook. She wasn't a manager.

Her dad spoke up again, always more in tune with Chrissy's moods than her mother had ever been.

"Don't worry, sweetie. We've got a couple of weeks and we will show you the ropes, hand over everything nice and official. We probably should have gotten you more involved a long time ago."

Chrissy thought so too, but she bit back the sarcastic reply, and simply put on her best daughter smile. "It's okay, Dad. We'll make it work. We always do."

Her mom was off and running again. "I just know you are going to do amazing things when you're in charge. You can finally make all those changes you've been nagging us about."

"What changes?" Chrissy didn't remember suggesting any changes. Sure, she'd thought about lots of things they could do to improve sales and get some extra traffic. But she didn't remember ever expressing them to her mom and dad. The restaurant was theirs. She was just waitressing until she found a husband and had a baby. Or at least, that's what she always felt her mom was saying.

Janine waved a hand. "Oh, you know, you wanted us to put up some fancy website."

"A Facebook page?" Chrissy laughed. She had suggested jumping on social media several years ago. Actually, she still thought it was a good idea.

"Sure, a Face page. Whatever. My point is you've

got lots of great ideas, sugar. And now the café will be yours! You've got tons of time to devote to the cafe, since you don't have any kids. Or even a boyfriend or anything."

Ignoring the barb at the end, Chrissy considered for a moment. It didn't sound too bad. Maybe this wasn't such a terrible thing after all. She took another bite of mashed potatoes, no longer feeling like she was going to throw up. She poured herself more wine, though. It was still a lot to take in.

Her parents lived about two blocks from Main Street and the cafe and Chrissy walked home that night in the rapidly cooling autumn air. Thanksgiving was in a few days and then it would be full-blown Christmas season. As she walked, her thoughts slowly drifted toward the café and what it would be like to know it was entirely hers.

Part of her always resented her ties to the café. Once, she'd been a dreamer. It hadn't been difficult to manage straight A's and advanced placement classes in high school. Chrissy went off to college with hopes of traveling the world as an international studies major. Instead, she returned home after the events of a dark night on the streets of Chicago. In some ways, Chrissy liked being a waitress. For one, and perhaps most importantly, it was safe. She enjoyed seeing everyone in town, teasing them about their affinity for pie or threatening to withhold their coffee refill. But deep inside her, the desire to do more, be more, and see more was still buried. This opportunity her parents were giving her? Maybe this was the answer. She could be Christine Mathes, business owner. Much better than Chrissy M, Waitress, the title currently displayed on her café nametag.

As long as she could remember, Chrissy had been a waitress. Even before she went to college, she was helping her parents at the cafe. The idea of being responsible for the entire restaurant had her pushing on her temples to ward off a headache. It was too much. She wasn't ready for this, and her parents' confidence was misplaced at best. What had ever possessed them to make this decision so quickly? Where was the fire? Overwhelming feelings of self-doubt and fear of failure took over her thoughts.

Until yesterday, Chrissy's life was a predictable routine of waitress, church, small group bible study and dreaming up vacations she wasn't confident she would ever take. The small savings account accumulating over the past five years would be more than enough to book her a flight almost anywhere in the world and explore for a week. As close as she'd been

—every detail planned and hotels and flights sitting in her online shopping cart—Chrissy remained unable to pull the trigger on one of her dream vacations. Her dreams of exploring the corners of the world had died in an alley in Chicago one November evening eight years ago.

Since then, no place felt safe. Only Minden.

Instead, she ordered travel guides and watched countless hours of The Travel Channel, planning theoretical vacations to India and Paris and Hong Kong. Every month when a portion of her budget went to her optimistically-named "Travel fund", Chrissy wished for her fears to be removed. But every month, she clicked the 'X' on the browser window without booking a trip.

As a business owner—the very thought still too foreign to dwell on—travel would pose an entirely different challenge. But it was still an intriguing thought. Business owner. Restaurateur. Chrissy could decide what to do. If she wanted, she could change the menu or paint the dreary beige walls. The café had been desperate for a new coat of paint for years but her parents didn't want to bother, content with how it was. Chrissy hadn't figured it was her place to bother, but now it was! Thinking of paint colors led her to the realization that the place needed new floors, too. Plus, new upholstery where the old was worn and ripped. She reached the door that would lead to her loft above the café, next to the glass window with a white sign announcing "Bud and Janine's Café" to the world, or at least to Main Street Minden. Instead of continuing upstairs, Chrissy pulled out her key to the café and went inside.

It was different like this. Chrissy didn't often come in before anyone else or stay long after the last customer was gone. The only light was coming through the big front windows from the streetlight outside. The smell of bacon and spicy chili lingered in the quiet air. Nearly every day of Chrissy's life had been spent in this café in one way or another. It had been her parents joy to spend their time there, cooking for and feeding their friends and to be the gathering place of their little town. Now, she studied the space with fresh eyes. Touches of her mom and dad filled the restaurant. Slowly, she imagined replacing them with touches of herself. The tired light fixtures replaced with cozy wood and cast-iron fixtures; the coffee-stained counter top with a modern granite. Chrissy loved relaxing with a cup of coffee and a friend here. She mentally replaced the tables in the front windows with couches and chairs meant for conversations or a book. Walking through the space, she trailed her fingers along surfaces and dreamed. The five thousand dollars she had saved for *someday* could be used today instead.

Chrissy finished her lap around the café and took one last look at the familiar room. As she pushed open the door, the bells interrupted the calm and quiet of the cool night. Chrissy hated those bells. *Maybe that will be my first change as owner,* she thought with a smile.

2

*L*ike he did most days, Todd Flynn stopped by Bud and Janine's for lunch. He tried to time his visits for when there wouldn't be many people around, either arriving before the lunch crowd or after. Todd knew Chrissy would be busy with other customers if he came at noon. Coming at 11:15, even if he wasn't quite hungry yet, ensured he would get more of her undivided attention. Todd and Chrissy had been friends a long time, having grown up just a few houses apart and close to the same year in school. Todd was drawn to her, and had been for years. Since she came home from college, it had only gotten worse. But they were friends. Todd could never do anything to jeopardize that relationship. So he came to see her several times a week and admired her way with people. Even now, as he watched her flit from table to table refilling waters and coffee and grabbing an empty plate to return to the kitchen, he thought she was beautiful. Chrissy floated, each move fluid and never wasted. She smiled warmly at every one, the same cheery smile she gave him when tesasing him about the pie being sold out, despite the early hour. Todd watched her from behind his coffee cup.

Surprising him, Chrissy sat down across from him at the booth when she brought his plate of food. A roast beef and swiss and a mountain of fries greeted him as he looked down. She was practically vibrating with excitement and it made Todd raise his eyebrow at her. He grabbed a French fry and pointed at her.

"Better spit it out, Chrissy, before you choke on it. I can tell when you've got news. You had this same look when you told me Charlotte and Luke got engaged." He rubbed a hand over his beard to conceal the smile and seem less enthralled with the woman sitting across from him.

"My parents are moving to Florida!" Chrissy squealed. Her jazzy hand gesture had Todd thinking she needed pom-poms to really get the point across. Before he could respond, she was talking a mile a minute. "I mean, at first I was really confused and scared, you know? They were all 'The café is yours now' and I was all 'uhh what?' But then my mom said something and it really got me thinking. I've got a ton of ideas for this place, Todd." She grabbed a fry from his plate and waved it around while she talked. "I'm going to make it so amazing. I want to replace the floors and paint the walls and replace the tables and countertop. Oh my gosh, I'm going to have to find a cook! How does one go about finding a cook? I'm going to rearrange the tables and maybe sell pastries by the register. Maybe I can find another baker who wants to sell their stuff here. Ooooh, I know – I could see if Ruth would bake for me on a regular basis, or if Margaret would do more than just pies."

His smile escaped and Todd tried his best to follow the flow of consciousness that was pouring out of his friend. It was adorable, and he tried to remember the last time he had heard her go on about something like this. He interjected, "Don't forget to breathe." She stopped talking and stuck out her tongue at him. He used this moment of silence to digest what she had said. "So, your folks are moving and they are leaving you the café? That's really awesome. Congratulations, Chris! You are going to do great. It sounds like you have a ton of ideas."

Todd's stomach flipped as he became the full focus of her attention. Chrissy looked at him with her big, baby blue eyes, not even subtle in her attempt to make them puppy-dog begging eyes. He sighed. "And I bet you want me to help with renovations." At the realization, Todd groaned. He was absolutely slammed for time between customers and school. But Chrissy didn't know about the school part. Of course she thought he'd have time for her. As it was, he didn't really have time to come here every day for lunch, but he did it anyway. And he knew he would do this.

Chrissy noticed none of this hesitation or lack of enthusiasm for her upcoming project and promptly got up from her seat across from him. She leaned over and grabbed his face with both hands and exclaimed, "I knew you'd understand! Thank you, thank you, thank you!" Her hands on his face made him wish he'd shaved his beard to feel her skin on his without the barrier. Then, she planted a kiss right on his forehead before flitting away to pick up an order from the window and deliver it to another table. Todd remained, picking at his lunch and trying to ignore the warm feeling that flooded him when she gave him her attention and gratitude. He'd do everything in his power to make her look at him like that again.

Todd analyzed all the projects he had open. A couple of pieces of custom furniture needed done by Christmas. The nativity stable for the church Christmas display needed to be complete just after Thanksgiving and he hadn't even started it. Plus, he had a paper due in Managerial Economics and a test to study for in Building Codes. *Maybe I can convince Chrissy to wait for renovations until after Christmas?* When he paid for his lunch, they agreed to meet at the café after it closed. The café was open for lunch every day and for dinner Wednesday through Saturday, so he could come by any time after four today. He mentally blocked out his time for the rest of day and texted Chrissy saying he would be by around six.

Todd ran a small business doing handyman jobs and small remodeling projects, but his true passion was doing custom woodworking projects. Recently, he designed and built a quilt rack for Miss Ruth, who had been a motherly figure to him his entire life. A new desk was in the works for his good friend, Luke, and his new fiancée, Charlotte. Charlotte was going to be working from home and Luke was surprising her with a home office in their new house. The stable for the nativity was the first large-scale custom piece everyone in town would see. He was so nervous he hadn't even been able to start working on it.

People in this town had known him forever. They'd known his father, too. How would people react the star football player, who had almost failed out of high school, actually trying to be something. It was one thing to be a handyman and fix some old lady's bathroom fan, or even to lay new tile. But to create something out of nothing but an idea? It seemed so much riskier. What if the stable turned out crooked or fell down before Christmas? *You'll never make something worthwhile, why would they ask you?* Todd shook his father's voice and its belittling words out of his head. He had four days until Thanksgiving and the stable was due on the Saturday after. He had to make it perfect. And for now, he had to forget about Chrissy—something easier said than done for him.

3

_T_he hours after lunch service died down and before closing time felt like a month. The two hours Chrissy had to wait for Todd after that? An eternity. She would fix something for dinner to kill the time. She told Todd to come hungry and tried to remember what he had for lunch, only remembering the French fries she had pilfered. Chrissy never ordered fries herself, afraid of hearing her mother's disapproval from the kitchen. Like most carbs, though, she loved them and couldn't resist if they were in front of her for too long.

She decided on pasta for tonight. After a brief debate of red or white sauce, Chrissy settled on a red cream sauce and started her work. They didn't serve anything like this at the café; pasta didn't really fit the menu. This was her own creation. Chrissy wasn't a bad cook, but she didn't love it—not like someone should love it to cook full-time. Her relationship with food was so muddled by her discomfort with her body and the guilt of knowing her appetite is why she could never seem to lose the twenty extra pounds. Tonight though, she wasn't letting those feelings color the mood. Chrissy was still so excited about the possibilities and eager to share those ideas with Todd. Tonight, she was making pasta with a heavy cream and sun-dried tomato sauce. *And I'm going to serve it with bread instead of a salad, so there, Mom.*

Todd came to the back door of the café, knowing that the front would be locked. When he walked in, he saw Chrissy absently stirring something on the stove. It smelled heavenly - garlic, basil, and other herbs Todd couldn't even begin to identify. In the industrial kitchen, she was clearly in her element - completely comfortable and relaxed. She leaned over to taste it and then grabbed something from a small dish near the stove and sprinkled it in with her fingers. There was an open bottle of white wine on the counter, near a cutting board that was now empty except for the onion skins and ends she hadn't used in the dish. She was wearing a white apron in the style of thousands of home cooks before her. The best part was that she was singing along to the radio. Badly.

As much as he wanted to stand here in the entrance admiring the picture she made, Todd knew he had a full night of schoolwork ahead of him after they finished here. So, reluctantly drawing her attention to his presence, he spoke over her off-key rendition. "Chrissy!"

She jumped, the spoon flying out of her hand and falling harmlessly to her feet, splattering something creamy over the floor and her shoes. Her hand flew to her chest and she scolded him, "Don't sneak up on a person like that, Todd Flynn. You about gave me a heart attack."

He shrugged. "Sorry. Maybe you should put bells on this door, too."

She laughed. Todd knew her disdain for the bells on the front door of the café. "Smart aleck. Are you hungry? I made pasta." Not waiting for an answer, Chrissy grabbed plates from where they sat on a metal rack to the left of the stove and began plating the food, giving generous portions to both of them. She pulled garlic bread from a foil wrapper near the back of the stove, and placed a couple of pieces on the edge of each plate.

"Sounds great, I'm starving." Todd could almost always find room to eat. He was still a big guy, naturally suited to his high school football position as a defensive lineman.

"Grab the wine, would you?" Chrissy gestured with an elbow as she held a plate in each hand.

They sat at the bar of the café and enjoyed their pasta. Todd complimented Chrissy on the food and she talked about her plans for the menu. She spoke with her hands, nearly spilling her glass of wine as she grew increasingly animated. Chuckling at her single-minded focus, Todd steadied the wobbling wine glass.

"I don't want to change everything. I know what sells here—your basic sandwiches and fries—but I think people would enjoy having a little more variety. Maybe a pasta special one night a week and add a couple better salads to the menu? I could easily dress up a couple of the items, like the BLT with some sort of aioli instead of plain mayo. It wouldn't be hard or expensive, but I think it would give the café a little more sophistication."

Todd watched the dreams dance in her eyes. "Do you think Minden can handle some sophistication?"

Chrissy sipped her wine and contemplated the question, thinking about the people who came to eat at the café now, mostly residents and people from the surrounding farms. "I think so. I think I can find a balance between the down-home cooking that everyone knows and loves but also cater to others. I bet we could even pull some travelers off the interstate if the reviews are good."

Interstate 70 ran about five miles south of Minden. It wouldn't be too far out of the way for someone traveling through the area if they wanted something other than fast food on their trip. Todd nodded, agreeing. "It would be nice to have something like this," he gestured to his nearly empty plate of pasta, "on the menu."

Chrissy beamed at the compliment. "Yes! But I need to make the look of the café match the new menu. And that's where you come in."

Todd finished his last bite of pasta and pushed his plate away. He turned on the barstool and surveyed the café. "Okay, tell me what you see."

Chrissy was only half done with her pasta, but she turned as well and began pointing out changes she'd like. "We have to do something about this floor. The old tile is so worn near the door, it isn't even a color anymore. I'm thinking wood, or something that looks like wood maybe?" Todd nodded and she continued. Chrissy stood while she talked,

"And I want to get rid of these big booths. They look like a 50's diner! I'm thinking one long bench that runs all along that wall, with smaller tables we can move around depending on the size of the group."

Todd interrupted, his mind trying to absorb the details. "How big do you want the tables? And do you want a wooden bench or one with a cushion?"

"Oh, I definitely want a cushion. I still want it to be comfortable and homey, so not just a plain wooden bench. As for the tables... I don't know. Maybe this big or so?" Chrissy held out her arms on the bar, reaching to Todd's other side with her left arm just past his plate. Her other arm reached just past her own plate. "And then maybe two feet wide or so?"

Todd tried to ignore Chrissy's arms creating a cage around him. "Okay, so you want two-person tables, where one person is on the bench and one person is in a chair across from them. I think you could get about eight tables along that wall without them being too crowded."

Chrissy moved back and then moved to the center of the dining room. "Great. And then I need some tables here, in the middle. I love round tables, but I know they aren't very practical. Maybe we could have a round table and then some rectangular tables in the rest of the space?"

Todd tried to build a picture in his mind, but was having some trouble. "I need to measure the space and then draw up some ideas. Anything else you want out here?"

Chrissy nodded. "I want some couches and chairs, for people to sit and have coffee or read a book. I'm thinking up by the front windows."

Todd thought about it. "I think it would better to do one set of couches in one window, but also have a table in one window, too. Then people walking by will see that you have both options."

"Great idea. Do you think one seating area with couches and chairs is enough?"

Todd shrugged. "I'm not sure. I'll draw it up a couple of ways and you can decide." He was thinking about the time he would spend on this and inwardly groaning. But, he was really excited about getting involved in a project of this scope. It might work as the final project required for a class he was in. "Let me grab my tape measure and write some stuff down. It's out in the car; I'll be right back. Then, you can tell me about the rest of the space."

When Todd returned, Chrissy was wandering around the dining room. "I forgot to tell you that I want to replace the light fixtures and paint the walls, too."

Todd's project scope continued to balloon. *Of course she does.* "That makes sense; it definitely needs it." Conscious of the ever-expanding budget, he asked, "Is the location of the lights okay, or do you want to move them around?"

Chrissy studied the existing light fixtures. Two big ceiling fans hung above the center portion of the dining room, and four smaller fixtures were spaced down either side. Despite their dated style, she thought the location would probably work. "I think the location is fine. At least they aren't fluorescent lights or anything like that!"

Todd agreed. "That's good. Moving the electrical would be pretty expensive. Which brings me to my next question." He got serious and walked toward her. "Chrissy, do you have the money for this?" After hearing about her grand vision for the place, he was concerned that she had no idea how much it was going to cost.

Her face fell. "Why, how much do you think it will cost?"

He did some quick mental math, talking her through his estimate. "Well, this space out here is about a thousand square feet, so you're looking at four grand for flooring, at least. The tables and chairs are expensive too. Maybe one-fifty each for the small tables, and two-fifty for the larger ones. So, maybe three grand for tables, plus fifty per chair." He watched the light in her eyes dim with every dollar amount. "Then you've got couches and light fixtures and the countertops." He softened his voice, dreading his role in breaking this news. "I think you're looking at thirty or forty thousand out here in the dining room."

Chrissy's face fell. "Oh wow, I didn't think it would be that much. I've only got a few thousand saved up." She thought about her travel fund.

Todd hated seeing that sad look on her face. "Hey, hey. It's okay. We can work something out, find ways to bring the cost down. If you help paint and some other jobs, that'll help." Also, it was a great way for Todd to finagle a little extra time with his best friend. He had no idea what he could have her help with beyond painting, but he was hoping she would agree.

She bit the inside of her cheek, and then look up at Todd with a hopeful smile. "Maybe I can get a loan? And I can definitely help paint." Chrissy said emphatically.

Todd was relieved. "A loan is probably a necessity, but I can help make sure you get approved." He drew a quick sketch of the dining room and began taking measurements of the space. He dictated them to Chrissy, who wrote them down on the correct place of his drawing. "When are you planning to close the diner for these renovations?"

"Shoot. I didn't even think about needing to close. How long will I be closed?"

"Well, obviously I'll have all the tables and chairs ahead of time, and most of the stuff will just need brought in. But we have to lay the floor and paint. I think a couple of weeks should do it."

"Oh man. Two whole weeks' worth of business lost? And when I need the money to pay for the renovation?"

"I know it sucks, but just think about how great it is going to be to have a grand re-opening party and show off the new space!" Todd tried to paint a bright, positive picture of the future for her. He wanted to make it happen for her.

Chrissy thought about it. "I could throw a party! And serve samples of some of the new menu items. Do you think New Year's would be too soon?"

Todd choked at the thought. "New Year's?" He croaked. "I'm sorry Chrissy. There is no way we can be done by New Year's. It's going to take at least two months for me to get that many tables and the bench for the East wall. That puts us at the end of January at the earliest." He considered it for a moment and then suggested, "How about a Valentine's Day opening?"

Chrissy, who had been disappointed at his initial response, smiled now. "I love it! Everyone can come to the party as part of their Valentine's Day dates! I'll make it cozy, romantic, and really show off the café's new feel."

They were done measuring the space now and settled back at the counter finishing the bottle of wine. Chrissy broke the comfortable silence. "I'm so thankful that you are doing this with me, Todd." When he didn't respond, she added, "Can I get you a piece of pie or something?"

Todd smiled at the offering, remembering their daily banter. "I wish I could, but I really need to get home and work on some things, including the drawings for your new space." He got up and put on his coat as they walked to the back door. After thinking about it, he was excited to draw up her space using some of the software was learning about in school. Plus, the more he considered the scope of her plans, he was confident it would fit the requirements of the project he had to complete for his Project Management class. He had been planning to use one of his furniture pieces, but this would be an even better assignment to try the methods on. As long as she could afford it.

"Okay. I am so excited to see them!" Chrissy leaned in and wrapped her arms around his torso. She squeezed him tightly and Todd closed his eyes and soaked in the feeling.

She let go too soon, the moment evaporating. He cleared his throat, thick with unspoken words and said instead, "And I can't wait to see your new menu. Thanks again for dinner."

4

Todd didn't make it back into the café for lunch on Tuesday or Wednesday. He spent hours on the 3-D software designing Chrissy's space. He'd used it in class but not on anything so complicated. He was learning so much that he hardly minded spending the extra time. Plus, he couldn't wait to show the 3-D renderings to Chrissy. He drew up the room and then created 3-D objects for the small tables, larger tables, and the round table he could copy and paste in different arrangements to see what worked. He looked up how much space was needed between tables, and even added light fixtures so the 3-D image looked convincing.

Todd wasn't sure the fabric colors or the wall color were what Chrissy would want, but he decided to bring his laptop over to her so she could play with them herself. It was Wednesday, which meant the café was open for dinner. He headed there around 7:30 and would hang around until it closed at 8. Tomorrow was Thanksgiving, which meant the café was closed until Sunday. He didn't have any classes until next week either. Hopefully, he and Chrissy could work on the restaurant some over the weekend. No plans for Thanksgiving Day. His family wasn't really the thankful type. Not that Todd would have wanted to go anyway. His dad died an angry middle-aged man from lung cancer, the result of smoking two packs a day since he was eighteen. His mom moved away and was "finding herself" somewhere on the west coast. The only thing he needed to do was finish the stable for the nativity. In between school-work and the 3-D renderings of Chrissy's bistro, he designed the stable and started working on it. Todd planned to finish it on Friday.

Todd knew he could go to Miss Ruth's house, but he didn't want to listen to Luke and Charlotte talk about wedding plans and act all lovey-dovey. He really was happy for them. Luke deserved happiness after his first wife died in a car accident so young. But it was difficult to see Luke capture twice in one lifetime what Todd had always wanted: a partner who knew him and loved him anyway. He said a quick prayer that God would take away his envy of his friend. While waiting for the cafe to close, Chrissy invited him to join her family for dinner on Thursday. Looking forward to spending more time with her, he gladly accepted.

After Todd finished dinner at the cafe and Chrissy's dad left, Todd pulled out his laptop and showed her what he had done. He was nervous. He'd spent too much time getting the details 'just right', but part of him was afraid Chrissy would laugh at him. Realistically, he knew she was too nice to do that, but the doubts always lingered.

Her reaction was more than he could have hoped for. "Holy smokes, Todd! How did you do this? It's amazing! I was expecting some pencil floorplan on a piece of lined notebook paper! Seriously, it's incredible. I didn't know you could do this." Chrissy was in absolute shock seeing her space with the new layout, flooring and lights in his 3-D software. "I don't even know what to look at. It's beautiful."

Todd ducked his head and smiled as he felt himself flush under his beard. "It's no big deal. Here, let me show you what I've got. Then we can start changing things." He showed her the two different layouts. One with two round tables, but only the one area with a couch and chairs. The other had two small seating areas with arm chairs and a couch, but there was only room for one round table in the center of the shop.

Chrissy bit her lip and Todd attempted to keep his eyes on the computer screen instead of her soft, pink lips. "Well, I think the one comfy area will be okay for now. Mostly, people use the café for meals, so the tables will be the most important thing. I guess if it starts having more of a hangout, coffee-shop feel as well, I could always change things up."

"That makes sense. What do you think about the design of the tables? I'm planning to use a painted black top with rustic-looking stained wood for accents. Then, I can tie the same rustic look into the bench along this wall. Painting most of the table black will mean we can use a little cheaper type of wood, plus it will be easier to clean between customers."

Chrissy was nodding along with everything he pointed out. "I think it looks great. When you say 'rustic-looking' wood, will it be more like a gray tone, then?"

"Exactly. Think about the old barn out past County Road 400 South, the one with half the roof missing? I'm thinking it will be that color." While he was studying, Todd watched a lot of the DIY Network, and he knew the barnwood aesthetic was very trendy right now. He just hoped Chrissy would like it.

"Yes! That would be perfect. I love how homey and cozy that would make the place feel."

"Okay, great. I'll try to get that set up. If we can't use true barnwood, we can improvise with something that looks similar. Now, I think a darker floor will look good with the black tables and light gray accents. Then you could balance it with a lighter color on the walls. Or, you could do darker on the walls and something lighter on the floor. It's up to you."

Chrissy considered it a little bit and looked at the existing floor, noticing the dark stains on the once-white linoleum. "Definitely a dark floor."

Todd laughed, "You got it. You don't have to pick them out yet, but you'll need to find exactly which light fixtures you want and to pick a paint color."

"Sounds great. I am so excited." Then, her smile dimmed. Now, I guess the only thing missing is the money to pay for this."

Todd nodded. "Let me think. Is there a loan on the café right now?" Chrissy bunched her lips up on one side and shrugged.

"I'm not even sure, actually," she admitted.

"Okay, well you'll want to find out if there is a mortgage and how much you still owe. It will probably make a difference about whether you can get a loan."

"What does that mean?"Chrissy gave him a puzzled look and he tried to explain.

"Well, it means the bank will give you back some of the value of the property in cash and they will own more of the café until you pay it back."

"Okay, I guess that makes sense. What do I have to do?" Chrissy took a deep breath, trying not to be overwhelmed.

"You need to figure out which bank your parents have the accounts through and go talk to them about a new loan, or a refinance on the existing mortgage."

He made it sound so easy. Chrissy shook her head, feeling helpless. "How do you know all this, Todd?"

He shrugged. "Just picked it up along the way, I guess."

Chrissy nodded, reassured. She hated being helpless. "Yeah. I guess I'm just so new at this whole running a business thing. But how hard can it be? After all, you do it." If Todd could run a business, she could do it too. Chrissy knew she could research and read up on all the things she needed to learn. Plus, she had Todd to help her.

Mentally grunting at the impact of the words, Todd suddenly leaned back from where he'd been inclined toward her and the computer. He absently rubbed his chest as though he could feel the barb that comment had left in his sternum. Not realizing the sting of her words, Chrissy simply continued exploring the 3-D rendition of her café, 'walking' between tables and looking at the space from the door, the kitchen and from every corner.

Todd was hurt but trying not to be. Running a business wasn't easy and he wanted Chrissy to appreciate that he worked hard to make his business successful. For awhile, he thought maybe she did see. But she only saw simple, stupid Todd like everyone else. Suddenly unable to sit there any longer, he jumped up.

"Okay, everything looks good here. I'll start working on the tables and the bench soon. And I'll bring some floor samples for you to look, too." Chrissy started at his sudden change of tone and demeanor.

"Okay, thanks so much. I don't know how you did all this," she gestured at the computer, "but it really helped me see how everything fit together. I can't wait to start drawing up the menu for the new place."

Todd was unable to speak, still hurting from her comment earlier. He packed up his laptop and left without another word, pretending not to notice when Chrissy held out her arms for a hug.

5

*T*odd texted Chrissy on Thanksgiving morning and told her he couldn't make dinner at her parents' house. He really needed to finish the stable for the nativity, as it was due Saturday night. While that was a good excuse, Todd was also nursing his hurt feelings from Chrissy's words the night before. She made it entirely clear how she saw him—helpful, but unintelligent. So, instead of enjoying a nice, warm Thanksgiving dinner, he decided to put it all out of his mind and do some work.

Todd had drawn up the stable he had designed for the nativity in the 3-D software and was very pleased with how it looked. Now, he just had to translate that design into the wood itself. In his mind, that was the easy part.

He started cutting the timbers with his miter saw. The stable was more complex than most, with three sections. The main section had a wide opening and a peaked roof, with beams connecting a lower cross post to the peak and the sides like a sunbeam. The sides were fenced all the way around with lower roofs that extended from the sides of the main portion. The roof was going to be thinner wood, but still planks – not sheet. He wanted it to look like a dressed-up version of an authentic stable. The wood was strong, sturdy oak and he would stain it a dark brown.

In order to transport the piece to the church and make sure they could store it for the rest of the year, he was making the stable in three parts. Even so, it was large. The church did a live nativity the week before Christmas, with real people and real animals, so the stable had to be at least large enough for two adults to sit inside with a baby. Plus, a couple of the animals would be in the side pens. To keep the weight down, the stable had no floor. He figured that was more realistic anyway. It was open on all sides, except the back of the center section, which was built like a fence panel with vertical planks of wood.

Todd blocked out everything else and got lost in the work he loved. Despite the cool weather, he was sweating in his workshop. He removed his sweatshirt and opened the door to let some cool air in. After he cut all the pieces he needed for the main section, he started to assemble the structure. Todd looked at his handiwork with pride when the section was complete. *I may be stupid, but I can make something worth appreciating.* Quickly, a voice inside him responded—more confident and less angry than his own.

You are wonderfully made and gifted beyond measure.

Todd closed his eyes, sinking into the reassurance of his Creator. He'd been studying and working on his confidence in devotionals for a long time, ever since he'd come to the realization that the lies he heard were from his earthly father and that the words of God were much different.

It hadn't been discussed as part of the project, but Todd realized the missing feature of his stable was the manger where baby Jesus laid. He quickly thought about how to make something and added it to his to-do list. The simple structure reminded him of the miracle of Jesus' birth and the humble circumstance of being born in a stable. Todd loved Christmas. He never had as a kid, not like other kids did. But since he became a believer, Christmas and Easter were his favorite holidays, since they meant so much. *Thank you for letting me build this stable. I hope it honors You. Forgive me for making the about me and my business.* Then, Todd got back to work, creating the two stable sections with a low fence on three sides.

CHRISSY and her parents had Thanksgiving Dinner along with a few of her aunts, uncles, and cousins. Todd's absence wasn't noticed by anyone but Chrissy. Janine insisted on hosting the gathering, even though they had already started packing away much of the house. So, Chrissy found herself digging through a box filled with dishes and packing paper.

"Mom, I can't find it!" Chrissy yelled to be heard over the ruckus 10-year-old boys chasing each other through the living room next to the parlor. The 'formal' living room had always been mostly off-limits to her as a kid and housed the piano and the nice couch. It was now home to stacks of boxes.

Her mom peered around the corner and rolled her eyes. "Not that box, Christine. I said it was the one labeled 'Glassware and Tupperware'. That one says 'Serving Dishes and Glassware'."

Chrissy responded sarcastically, "I'm not sure how I could have made such an *obvious* error." She began repacking the box she had mostly unpacked without finding the gravy boat. According to Janine, the world might end if they served dinner without a gravy boat. Attempting to distract her mother and change the subject, she asked "How is dinner coming? I'm starving!"

"Dinner's almost ready, sweetie. I think your father really outdid himself this year. Maybe you should grab a healthy snack now, so you aren't tempted to each too much later. I've got some apples in the fridge leftover from the apple crisp."

Chrissy just nodded and said, "Sure, mom. That's a great idea." Rolling her eyes as she dug through the second box of dishes, she tried not to disturb things. Triumphantly holding up the gravy boat out to her mother, she said, "Here, you take this back to the kitchen and I'll get this packed back up." *An apple? That's not likely. Especially when I know mashed potatoes are waiting just around the corner.* Despite her internal monologue of sassiness, Chrissy reminded herself not to over-indulge. *Lots of veggies.*

And skip the sweet potato casserole. You don't really like it anyway.

When dinner was finally served and her father had said a blessing over the meal, Chrissy stood in line and filled her plate. As usual, she ran out of room far before she reached the end of the counter and ended up with her turkey and roll thrown on top of an already full plate. She avoided carrying her plate past her mother and found a place at the table, quickly relaxing and enjoying the conversations with her family .

THE FRIDAY AFTER THANKSGIVING, Mark texted Todd and invited him over to watch the rivalry college football games that were on. Mark told funny stories from family dinner with his brothers the day before. When all five of the Dawson boys were together, you never knew what was going to happen. Todd had even played football briefly with Mark's oldest brother, Daniel who now played for the Revolutionaries, an NFL team from Boston.

Sometimes, Todd wondered what it would have been like to grow up in a family like that—brothers to play with and a mother and father who loved Jesus and their kids with nearly equal passion and consistency. It was the kind of family Todd wanted to have someday. Mark was the clown of the family, always cracking jokes and telling stories. His ability to balance his intellectual side with his funny side brought only admiration from Todd. Todd had to figure the students loved him, and based on the stories that Mark told about the antics of his students, he really enjoyed teaching.

Despite the lazy Friday vacation plans of football and foot, Mark was stylishly dressed, with a collared button-down and his hair gelled carefully into the trendy style Todd mostly saw on television. When Todd saw Mark, he glanced down at his own Levi's and Carhartt jacket. He raised an eyebrow at his friend, but Mark just rolled his eyes and opened the door wide. Todd knocked the mud off his boots before walking in and took them off just inside the door.

Mark and Todd devoured the Thanksgiving leftovers Mark's mom sent home with him. The halftime show started and Mark turned down the annoying voices of the hosts. "What have you been working on lately? I feel like I've been talking the whole time." Todd pulled out the pictures of the stable on his phone and showed Mark. Then, he started talking about Chrissy's renovation.

"She's got this huge vision for the restaurant now that it belongs to her. It's going to be really awesome." Todd's excitement couldn't help but show in his voice.

Mark nodded. "That'll be cool. Downtown Minden has a lot to offer, but I feel like it can support a restaurant with a different feel to it. Maybe it will help get some other business into the empty spaces." There were several thriving businesses on Main Street, but there were a couple of empty store fronts, too. Todd wondered if his woodworking business would ever find the need for a store front. He could display samples of larger pieces and sell smaller things, like cutting boards or wooden signs, out of an inventory. Before his mind wandered too far, he pulled himself back into the conversation.

"Exactly. I'm pretty excited to do this project. I think it will end up being the biggest solo project I handle as General Contractor. Plus, I'm making all the tables and chairs for the space."

Mark recognized the milestone. "Dude, that's huge! Congrats, man. Your woodworking business is going to take off for sure. Miss Ruth was absolutely beside herself telling all the ladies at church how wonderful the quilt rack you made was."

Todd filled with pride. "That's cool. I'm glad she liked it."

Mark nodded. "She definitely did. Chrissy is really lucky to have you as a friend to do this project for her."

Todd's smile fell a bit, and he nodded absently, focused on the game as it kicked back off. "Yep."

Mark burst out laughing, "Dude, you've got it so bad." Todd hung his head as Mark continued, "Does she have any idea how you feel about her?"

Todd shook his head. "I don't think so. At least, I've never told her. We flirt and we talk but there's no way. She'll never go for a guy like me."

"What do you mean *a guy like you*?" Mark gave him a genuinely confused look.

"You know. Like *me!* A dumb-jock. She was practically valedictorian." Todd tipped his head back on the couch cushion and stared at the ceiling. Anything to avoid looking at his friend and seeing pity in his eyes.

Mark clicked his tongue. "Oh man, you've got a seriously backwards view of yourself. Personally, I think she'd go for you. But you've got to make the first move. Girls like Chrissy? They don't put themselves out there. Maybe she's waiting for you. I mean, it's not like she's been dating much over the last few years!"

Todd considered that. It was true. Chrissy hadn't dated anyone. She was beautiful, funny, and kind. She loved Jesus and people more than almost anyone he knew. He could think of a handful of guys who would jump at the chance to take her on a date. He'd even heard a few of them ask her while she waited on their table at the cafe, but she'd always turned them down with a smile. Todd had never really taken the time to wonder why in the midst of his relief. Even though he never thought he was good enough, the thought of her dating someone else always made him slightly nauseous.

Todd determined to change the subject. Enough about Chrissy. It would never happen. They were just friends. "What about you, Mark? Anybody caught your eye lately?"

Mark sent his own glance heavenward. "Ugh, now you sound like my mom. Nope, nothing. I wish there was, it'd be easier. You know how many ridiculous Valentine's I get from infatuated 6th grade girls? Sometimes I think about wearing a wedding ring at school just to discourage some of them a bit. Girls these days are definitely not timid." He let out a mock shudder and Todd laughed.

The game was back on, but Todd didn't pay much attention to it. He let the conversation fade as he sat in the recliner to let the thoughts of Chrissy and the echo of Mark's words roll through his mind. Did he really have a shot with Chrissy? What would it take for her to see him as more than a friend? Maybe this renovation was his chance to show Chrissy who he really was and convince her to give him a chance.

6

When Charlotte requested Chrissy take a day trip with her to Indianapolis to shop for a wedding dress, Chrissy was torn. It would be amazing to get away from the cafe for a day, having spent nearly every waking moment there since she found out her parents were moving. But she also hated to leave Minden. Indianapolis wasn't as big as Chicago, and it was just a day. She'd be with her friends the entire time. Convincing herself was easier than she expected. Maybe fear was losing its hold on her.

When Charlotte drove up in her Jeep, Ruth was in the passenger seat. Chrissy climbed in the back and handed to-go coffee cups to Charlotte and Ruth. A coffee for herself remained in the styrofoam drink caddy she had carried out. In the backseat, she was greeted by a small present wrapped in pale blue paper with her name on it.

"Well, go on. Open it." Charlotte put the SUV in park and turned around from the driver's seat, eager to watch Chrissy open the gift.

Chrissy peeled back the shiny paper and opened the plain white box. Nestled inside was a delicate bracelet with a series of numbers on it. Chrissy puzzled at them for a moment, before recognizing them—GPS coordinates. Under the bracelet was a small card that read "It hasn't been long since we first met, but you are a friend I will never forget. Will you be my bridesmaid?"

Chrissy squealed in excitement. "Oh, Charlotte! Of course I would love to be your bridesmaid. That's so exciting!"

"I'm so glad. Those coordinates are to Bud and Janine's cafe. It's where we first met, and I know it is important to you! Ruth here is going to be my Maid of Honor," Charlotte explained with a grin and Ruth blushed.

"I don't know why she'd want an old lady like me standing up there, but I couldn't say no! It's whatever the bride wants, right?" Ruth looked absolutely tickled that Charlotte had asked her to be a part of the wedding, even beyond the wedding planning that they were already tackling.

"It's going to be so much fun!" Chrissy knee bounced and she started thinking of what they could do as a wedding shower. Maybe even a bachelorette party. On the trip to Indianapolis she learned that Luke was going to ask Todd to be the Best Man and Mark to be a groomsman. She made a mental note to follow up with Todd to coordinate dates for the parties.

They spent the entire trip talking about the wedding and what Charlotte would be looking for in a wedding dress. It didn't surprise Chrissy that they were making the trip to the city to go shopping. Terre Haute didn't seem to fit Charlotte's personality. She would look great in a designer gown and had the body to pull it off. And despite the small-town wedding, Chrissy knew that Charlotte wouldn't look out of place at all, regardless of what style she chose.

They drove to the north side of Indianapolis, to the wealthiest suburb, and started shopping. At the first shop, Charlotte tried on dresses of all different styles, ball gowns, A-lines, and mermaid. They compared necklines and sleeve styles, debating whether it would be too cold to wear a strapless gown. Chrissy said they could crank the heat up in the church and that Charlotte could wear a coat or cape any time she needed to be outside. Nothing at the first store felt like "the dress" though, so they took a quick break for lunch before going to the next bridal store. After explaining what they thought about styles she'd already tried on, the stylist pulled a hanger from the rack.

The stylist held up the white fabric and draped it artfully across her arm. "This is one of my all-time favorite dresses." Then, with a knowing smile, she added, "I think it is going to look absolutely lovely on you." Charlotte eyes were wide, studying the beaded lace with anticipation. She agreed to try it on and left Ruth and Chrissy seated on a small sofa in front of the raised platform and wall of mirrors.

Charlotte walked out, lifting the dress with both hands as it was clearly not made for her 5′3″ frame. Her face was warm and excited; her eyes bright. The scoop neckline with off-the-shoulder sleeves of delicate lace, and a fitted bodice with a beaded lace overlay created a stunning image. The beading trailed off near the waist and fingers of lace trailed down to mid-thigh where the dress still clung to Charlotte's subtle curves. From there, the smooth satin draped loosely to the floor, with a short train in the back.

The attendant helped adjust the length of the skirt so the group could see the effect. It was almost a mermaid-style dress but the effect was very subtle. The fitted portion at her thighs was not skin tight and the bottom portion wasn't as fluffy as the dresses they had tried on previously.

Chrissy was the first to speak. "Charlotte, you look like a celebrity on the red carpet." Chrissy let her admiration color her voice.

Charlotte smiled and admitted, "I feel like one, too."

Ruth wiped under her eye with the tissue she'd been carrying around all morning. "I think it's lovely, dear. Luke is going to absolutely lose his mind," she choked out. They all laughed at that comment.

"I love the sleeves!" Chrissy continued expounding on the good qualities of the dress, in case Charlotte wasn't sold.

Ruth nodded. "I agree. It is the perfect combination of traditional and modern—just like you and Luke."

"I never thought I would go for lace, but this feels perfect." At that, Charlotte let a tear slip and nodded. "This is the one."

Chrissy, Ruth, and the attendant cheered. Then, the stylist continued, "Let's get all your measurements so that we can get the dress ordered. When is the wedding?"

Charlotte looked nervous, but lifted her chin and spoke confidently. "It's January 27th." Chrissy's eyes widened. She hadn't even known the date.

The stylist's eyes widened. "Oh boy. That's only, what, seven weeks away?" She clicked her tongue. "We will have to do a rush order on this. It's an extra ten percent. Is that going to be okay?"

Charlotte nodded. "Oh yes, I'm just glad you can make it happen!"

The stylist looked relieved the bride wasn't unreasonable. "Alright, great. While we get your measurements for the order, let's have you ladies pick out something for the bridesmaids!" The attendant spoke with enthusiasm and Chrissy tried to be optimistic about it as well.

Charlotte must have seen the reservation on her face. She stepped close and looked at Chrissy's eyes. Reaching for Chrissy's hands, she spoke softly but firmly. "Chrissy, you and Ruth are the only two who will be up there with me. I don't expect you to wear matching dresses. Just pick out something that coordinates with each other and the wedding colors. Whatever dress you are comfortable in. You are going to look fabulous." Charlotte squeezed Chrissy's hands before dropping them and turning to step onto the dais to let the stylist take her measurements.

Chrissy nodded and fought the thick feeling in her throat. How did Charlotte know exactly what she was thinking? Glad she wouldn't have to squeeze into something designed for a body like Charlotte's, Chrissy headed toward the bridesmaid section. Ruth flipped through the racks with her. When she tried to imagine Ruth in some bridesmaid dress typically worn by 20-somethings, they both laughed. After a few discouraging episodes in the dressing room with samples she couldn't even zip, Chrissy tried on an A-line gown that was ruched on the side. It had a corset-top with a ribbon to lace up in the back, which helped her feel a bit better about her size. The ruching and the corset certainly seemed to help disguise her slightly squishy middle section. Her dress didn't have long sleeves, but it did have wide lace shoulder straps connected to give the illusion of a V-neck. She ordered it in an icy blue fabric that coordinated with what they picked out for Ruth. Ruth shopped in the Mother-of-the-Bride section of the shop and was able to find a lovely dress in Silver and Pale blue. It even had a lace bodice and sleeves that mirrored the dress that Charlotte would be wearing.

After everyone was measured and the stylist reassured Charlotte everything would be ready in five weeks to come back for alterations, they left. Still chattering about the success of the shopping trip and the beautiful dresses, they pulled into a drive-thru coffee shop to grab a pick-me-up for the drive home. Chrissy sipped her peppermint mocha and dreamed about her own wedding dress. Would she ever get to wear one? Would it still be white? She always felt like her own indelible scarlet 'A' prominently displayed on her clothes, even if she was the only one to see it. Since her improbable wedding day would still be years in the future, she shook off her depressed thoughts and refocused on the conversation happening between two of her favorite people in the front seat. Tomorrow would be back to the cafe, and the continuing struggle of trying to learn everything she could in a short time. There was so much to do—but for now, she just sat back and enjoyed the last hours of their Girls' Day Out.

7

*I*t had been two weeks since Chrissy was officially given ownership of the café. She felt like she was drinking from a firehose—trying to learn the process of ordering supplies, keeping track of the books for taxes, calculating the payroll. Running the cafe was turning out to be more involved than she imagined. With all the stress, her fingernails were bitten to the nub. Plus, she still hadn't had time to look for a new cook. Honestly, Chrissy didn't even know where to start. She started with the easiest, which was a sign imaginatively printed with "Hiring Cook. Apply inside." Unfortunately, Chrissy had no real hope it would work.

Racking her brain, she pulled up the Craigslist page for Terre Haute and posted a job on the board.

Terre Haute was about forty-five minutes from Minden, so maybe someone living between the two places would be looking for a job. Luckily, Margaret from the bakery provided the pies the café had served for years, and Chrissy was hoping she'd be willing to add cookies and other small desserts to her workload.

Chrissy was texting Charlotte about wedding plans when she realized the obvious. Charlotte had worked in recruiting and hiring for a big executive firm before moving to Minden. Now, it looked like she would be working for a recruiting firm that specialized in hiring pastors for large churches. *Charlotte probably knows how I can find someone. And how to actually interview them.* So, Chrissy asked Charlotte for help. Glad to be marking one thing off from her pile of things to do, she sighed and turned her attention back to the inventory sheet. Sure, she'd done inventory before. That part was easy. But what happened with the sheet after inventory was done was more confusing. Her dad tried to explain his system but it didn't make sense.

"I always order enough to have ten loaves of Texas Toast in stock," Bud explained.

Chrissy pushed further. "Why ten loaves?"

Bud looked up and ran a hand over his chin.

"Well, I know we use about seven loaves every week for French Toast and garlic bread. So, I figure if I have ten at all times, I'll never run out."

That doesn't help, Dad! She wanted to yell. Instead, she took a breath and probed further. "Okay, but how do you know you use seven loaves a week?"

Bud hesitated and then shrugged. "You know, I don't know. I guess I just figured it out over time." Then he laughed, in the carefree manner he usually carried. "I probably ordered too much or not enough early on and then had to throw some away or ran out." He gave Chrissy a warm, reassuring smile. "You'll figure it out, sweetie."

Despite her father's faith, Chrissy was not so confident. What if she added something to the menu and then ordered too much of it and wasted a bunch of money? Or what if she didn't have enough and everyone got mad because she didn't have what they wanted? She felt her blood pressure rise each time her parents admitted another thing they didn't track on paper, just knowing off the top of their heads what was needed.

Chrissy squeezed the bridge of her nose and thought about what else to ask. "Who do we even order from?"

Bud's face lit up as he was able to answer her

question. "From Parker Foods." He pulled a small stack of business cards from the center draw of the desk, flipping through it until he found the one he wanted. "Here's the company info. Their sales rep usually comes by about once every two or three months. Otherwise, you just give your next order form to the driver who brings your order. They are the company we get all our frozen foods—fries, chicken strips—and the pantry goods; like the bread, mashed potatoes, and beans for chili and such. They also have pretty good frozen soups."

Some of Chrissy's unease faded. She knew how much of what they served came frozen. She didn't like it, but it made cooking easier when she had to fill in. "Okay, I think I can manage that."

Bud flipped through the business cards. "Oh, but we get our meat from Thomas's Farm out by Greencastle. We get produce from them too." He handed her two cards. "And once a month we get coffee from Green Valley."

Chrissy just laid her head into the crook of her arm on the desk and groaned. She would never keep all this straight. She'd probably forget to order from one of the suppliers and not have milk or something. Chrissy sat up abruptly. "Who do we get our milk and eggs from?"

"That comes from Parker Foods, too."

Chrissy nodded and resolved to figure this out. *I can do this.* "Maybe I should write this all down."

ON SATURDAY NIGHT after the café closed, Chrissy was still trying to make sense of it. When Todd finally came to see her again—he'd skipped lunch all week—she was trying to get the Parker Foods order ready for the next day. She didn't even know what he was already bringing on the truck tomorrow and it was throwing her off. Chrissy shot Todd a grateful smile when he walked in.

Todd showed her the flooring options he had selected. He'd gone to a flooring specialty store in Terre Haute, wanting more selection than the big box home improvement store would offer. Todd chose some square tile vinyl that looked like ceramic. He also had two varieties of vinyl tile that were long and skinny, like a wood plank. All the flooring he had chosen was commercial-grade, so he knew it would hold up for a long time with all the traffic. Plus, it was inexpensive – much less than doing real tile or engineered wood.

Chrissy went with the least expensive. Though,

she claimed it was because she liked the look of it the best. Todd liked it too; the fake wood looked 'too' unreal, in his opinion. And the 4" x 12" shape would give some visual interest instead of the usual square tile. He said he would get it ordered and that it would probably arrive sometime after Christmas, in plenty of time for them to install it in February.

Todd studied her tight, drawn smile—so different than the carefree, bright grin he was so used to and asked, "Okay, Chris. What's wrong?"

"It's nothing. No big deal." But her eyes shimmered as she looked away.

"Come on, you can tell me." Todd wanted her to lean on him. She was always independent and strong. Not that she saw herself that way. But she didn't complain. Chrissy never gave up.

She hung her head and admitted, "I don't think I can do this, Todd. There's too much for one person. And I don't know how to do anything. I'm going to order too many eggs or not enough eggs and then Jim Platts won't be able to get his omelet next week because we won't have any eggs. And I'll forget to order coffee because it's from a different supplier and we won't have any coffee and what is a café without coffee?" She wailed this last question as tears spilled over her cheeks and she laid her face on his shoulder and sagged.

Todd rubbed her back and whispered to her. "Shhh. Shhhh. It's okay. You can do this, Christine Mathes. You are smart and capable and you can do anything you set your mind to. And if you don't order enough eggs for next week, you will run to Greencastle after closing and buy a shopping cart full from the Apple Mart.

She sniffed and lifted her head, "I can do that?"

He smiled. "Of course, you can do that. It's your café. You can get your eggs wherever you want to. Now, you might pay a little more to cover an ordering mistake, but Jim can still get his omelet in the morning."

He wiped the tears from her cheeks and held her face. "You can do this, Chris. I believe in you."

And he did. Chrissy was one of the most intelligent people he'd ever met. In high school, she'd always done well in classes. She studied her Bible and was never afraid to tackle hard subjects in the Sunday School classes they went to. Todd forced himself to look away from her red-rimmed blue eyes. Chrissy was so close to him right now, he could duck his head and kiss her without so much as a step.

The urge to do so was almost unbearable.

Now wasn't the time, though. Todd wasn't quite sure where this crisis of confidence was coming from, but he wasn't going to let her get away with it. "Come on. Let me help you with that order form tonight. And then, this weekend we can create a system for you to help keep track of everything. That would help, right?"

"I guess so. Part of what is so frustrating is that my parents just winged it and know so much after thirty-five years that I don't think I'll ever know."

"You'll get there. And they are always just a phone call away, okay?" He gently rubbed her shoulder.

"You're right. Thanks, Todd. You're a great friend."

Yep. That's me. A great friend. He sighed, wanting to be so much more. *Maybe once I have my degree, she'll see me differently. Maybe I'll be good enough then.*

8

_T_hey weren't planning to tackle the ordering system until Friday night, but Todd stopped by after the cafe closed on Thursday night anyway. The snow was falling lightly, just barely covering the sidewalks of Minden with a thin layer of white. The air had a bite to it and Todd nuzzled the cozy warmth of his scarf with his mouth and cheeks. The scarf had been a gift from his newest friend and the newest addition to their little town – Charlotte. Apparently, she had taken up crochet since moving away from the city. The thought of her sitting in the cabin and crocheting made him smile. When Charlotte first came to town, she was all designer clothes and big-city sass.

For a moment, Todd watched Chrissy through

the window of the diner. She stood by the counter, pulling what appeared to be Christmas decorations from a plastic tote. A smile lit her face at a couple of the pieces and some made her tip her head back in laughter. Todd reveled in the peace and joy on her face as she continued, unaware of his presence. He hesitated to knock, knowing how stressed out she was lately, and knowing more time with Chrissy would only make it harder to be nothing more than friends. Before he could turn and walk back home, Chrissy noticed him and enthusiastically waved him in.

Chrissy gave him a quick hug once he was inside. "I'm so glad you're here! I was just getting ready to hang up decorations, but now that I think about it – it really feels like something that shouldn't be done alone, you know?" She looked around at the restaurant. "We should have had the cafe decorated weeks ago, but with everything else going on, my parents never got around to it." Suddenly shy, she quickly backpedaled. "I mean, if you can't stay, it's totally not a big deal. I didn't mean to assume you wouldn't have plans or whatever." She was embarrassed at her enthusiastic invitation before he'd even said two words.

"Actually, I'd love to help." Chrissy wouldn't know it, but no matter how much work was piled up at home for him to do—including starting on her custom tables—there was nothing he would rather do than spend time with her. Even if the time was spent scraping gum off the bottom of desks, as they'd done together in 10th grade detention, it would be the highlight of his day.

Chrissy clapped her hands together in excitement. "Great! I was just going through the first box, but there are two more in the storage room in the back that I couldn't reach."

Todd headed that way. "No problem, I'll grab them." He came back with two heavy totes stacked in his arms. By that point, he had committed to carrying them both. Despite the burning in his arms and thighs, his pride wouldn't let him put one down now.

Todd set them on the floor and tried not to sound winded. Christine was by the front door, hanging a wreath on the inside of the glass. She came back to the counter and opened one of the boxes. Pulling out several small candle holders decorated with garland and gold ribbon, she turned them over in her hands and turned down one corner of her mouth.

"What's wrong?" Todd asked.

"These usually go on the tables. But they are getting pretty worn out. We've probably used these same ones for fifteen years. I think I remember making them with my mom." Chrissy smiled at the memory, and placed the decorations on the closest tables. "I think I'll use them this year, one last time. But I'll have to find or make something new next year that fits our new feel."

Todd marveled at her sensitive heart. It was fitting to honor her parents role in this place one more year. "I think that's a great idea."

For an hour or so, Todd helped Chrissy hang garland, wrap the picture frames on the wall in Christmas paper, and set up a small tree by the cash register. He turned on Christmas carols using his phone and they hummed and sang along.

After one song ended, Todd turned to Chrissy and asked, "What do you get if you eat Christmas decorations?" He waited a beat and then answered his own question. "Tinsel-itis!" He delivered the punchline with gusto and Chrissy burst out laughing at the ridiculous pun. Encouraged, Todd threw out another. "What's the best Christmas present ever?" This time, he waited for her response.

"I don't know. What?" Chrissy raised her eyebrows at him with a skeptical smile.

Todd paused for effect. "A broken drum! You can't beat it." Again, Chrissy laughed and his heart sang in response. He made her laugh. And it was his favorite sound in the world. Chrissy was standing on a chair hanging something above the entrance to the kitchen.

Thinking she might need help, Todd walked over and stood before her just as she hopped down from the chair. Steadying her with both hands on her waist, he looked up to see what she'd been hanging.

In a quiet voice, he asked, "What body part do you only see at Christmas?"

Nearly breathless from his close proximity, she responded in a whisper. "Which one?"

"Mistletoes," he said with his eyes twinkling as they returned to hers. Then, because he wasn't sure he'd ever have as good an excuse as standing under the mistletoe—he leaned down and kissed Chrissy.

It was a brief kiss, just the light pressure of her lips against his. But his hands tightened on her waist, even as he lifted his head. Todd's eyes stayed closed as he reveled in the moment, not wanting it to shatter. It was everything he'd imagined.

For years, he'd dreamed about a moment like this. He'd wished for it and denied the desire for as long as he could remember. Finally, his eyes flicked open and found hers. Chrissy was touching her lips with her fingers. Her eyes held so many questions.

"Todd?"

He considered apologizing, of excusing the kiss as a simple obligatory tradition. But he didn't want to apologize. What he wanted was to kiss her again. And again. "Yeah Chris?" Still, he held her waist in his strong hands.

Chrissy dipped her head for a second before raising her eyes to his once more. "Do it again?"

At those three simple words, his heart soared and he gladly fulfilled her request. With permission granted and years of pent up passion threatening to explode, Todd captured her mouth with his. He pulled her closer and was rewarded with her hands on his upper arms. One hand slid up to his neck and fingered the hair curling slightly at his collar and fingering the soft hair of his beard.

Todd opened his mouth and pressed forward, thrilled when she responded by parting her lips slightly. As perfect as the first kiss had been, this was more. Softer. Closer. Hotter. Chrissy's sweet taste overcame his senses and nothing outside of their embrace existed. Todd's pulse thundered and he moved one hand from her waist up to her hair, holding her face close to his, even as he lightened the kiss and eventually pulled away. They both took a ragged breath, still caught in the moment as Rudolf the Red-nosed Reindeer played merrily in the background.

Chrissy was the first to speak, clearing her throat and stepping out his embrace. Finding it safer to talk about anything but the kiss, she looked up at the mistletoe. "Every year, my dad would hang mistletoe over the door to the kitchen. Then he'd find every excuse to bump into my mother under it." She smiled at the memory. "Mom always tried to throw out the mistletoe after Christmas, but Dad would either rescue it from the trash or buy another one, I guess. I'm going to miss them so much."

Todd stroked a hand down her hair. "I know. I'm going to miss them too. But I have to say - I'm a big fan of your Dad's little tradition."

9

*A*fter the café closed on Friday night, Todd came to the back door and found Chrissy. He could tell she'd had a crazy day at work by the lopsided ponytail she hadn't bothered to fix. Their plans for working tonight on her organization system wouldn't exactly be relaxing, so Todd convinced her to take a walk before heading to her loft. They hadn't spoken of the kiss after it had happened last night, and Todd sensed no desire in Chrissy to bring it up tonight. That was fine with him, but he was sure hoping for a repeat performance if he could finagle one.

They walked through town, enjoying the Christmas lights decorating the store fronts and the lighted garland wrapped around the streetlights.

Todd held his arm out for her and warmed when she tucked her hand in it as they strolled along. They walked by the church and checked out the nativity which had been set up last weekend. Todd had eagerly helped the volunteers put it together, pride swelling in his chest as friends slapped his shoulder and shook his hand. The plastic characters inside the display would be replaced by live people and animals for one night during the week leading up to Christmas. When they stopped to take a closer look, Chrissy noted that the church had definitely upgraded from the old stable—a rickety, small structure of two by fours. Todd swallowed nervously and told her, "I made the new stable." The pride in his voice was disguised by a layer of self-doubt. What would Chrissy think? Wide eyes of shock and joy stared back at him when he finally looked up from his boots.

Chrissy's looked back at the stable. "Seriously? You made that? That's amazing, Todd."

Todd beamed, standing up straighter. "Thanks. It's been my favorite project so far. But I think your tables and bench are going to take over that spot soon."

Chrissy's brow wrinkled. "Wait, what do you mean?"

He looked at her, confused. "What do you mean, 'What do I mean'? I'm really excited to make your tables and the bench at the café."

Understanding lit her eyes. "Oh my gosh. I didn't even realize you were planning to make all that. I thought you were just going to order it somewhere!"

Todd tilted his head, "Do you not want me to make it?"

"Of course, I want you to make it." Chrissy shook her head at the misunderstanding. "It's going to be so beautiful, I just didn't really know you could do all that. I thought you could help with the renovations, I didn't intend to force you to make fifteen tables!"

Todd shrugged. "It's honestly what I love to do. And I think the custom furniture is going to look great in your space."

"Judging by how great this stable looks, I can't believe I'm lucky enough to have a friend with so much talent who is willing to do something like that for me."

Todd turned her to face him and said seriously, "It's my pleasure. Chris, I am so excited to be a part of you chasing your dreams with the bistro." Then, to remind her he didn't want to be just a friend; Todd leaned down to kiss her. The cold of her nose on his cheek contrasted with the warmth of her mouth on his. Chrissy leaned into him and tightened her grip on his arm where she still held it. A gust of cold wind grabbed his scarf and it whipped up to hit them both in the face, forcing them to pull apart. Swatting it away with a laugh, Todd pulled away and tucked Chrissy against his side again to lead them down the sidewalk back towards the cafe.

The warmth from her praise and the kiss followed him all the way back to the café where they headed up to her loft with copies of the order forms, inventory sheets, and the menu. Chrissy also grabbed the last two weeks' worth of receipts.

"Where do you want to start, Chrissy?" Todd wanted this to be her project and resisted his natural instinct to take over.

"Let's start by creating something to track the inventory electronically." Chrissy spoke with confidence and Todd nodded.

"That's a great idea. Do you think a spreadsheet would work?"

"I think so. Then I could take inventory on paper, and just type in the numbers on the spreadsheet. Oh, someday I could just take inventory on, like, a tablet or something."

"See, now you're thinking!" They got Chrissy's laptop fired up and created a spreadsheet. Chrissy typed the inventory items onto the sheet while Todd read them to her. Her dad said he had created the inventory sheet a long time ago, but since then had just been making photocopies of it every few months. "Texas Toast. Hamburger Buns. Dinner Rolls. Rye Bread." Her dad had apparently organized it by item type as well, though there were several handwritten items at the bottom.

It took a while to get all the items onto the spreadsheet.

"Okay, now what?" Todd asked.

"Well, how I decide if I have enough of a certain item after doing inventory?" Chrissy was getting into the process now. She was eager to make her restaurant succeed.

"Okay, well, let's think about this. How often do you get a shipment?"

"Well, Dad said that Parker Foods comes by every Wednesday. And meat and produce comes twice a week from Thomas's. And coffee comes once a month."

"See? You are doing great." Todd thought for a minute how he would organize the system and suggested, "Maybe you should organize the inventory by vendor AND by category? And you could list a 'target' amount for each item based on how often it gets delivered and how much you sell."

Chrissy's eyes lit up,"Oh, you mean like how my dad says he always orders back to have ten loaves of Texas Toast in stock."

Todd nodded. "Yeah. You just have to figure out what the target for each item should be."

"Ugh, that's going to take forever."

"I'll be here the whole time," he said with a smile. "Any idea how many hamburger buns you need each week?"

Chrissy closed her eyes and tried to count. "Maybe fifteen per lunch shift and twenty for each dinner shift? So.... fifteen times seven and twenty times four, what is that?"

Todd spoke quietly to himself. "Eighty. One-oh-five." Then louder he said, "One-hundred eighty-five hamburger buns."

They went on like this for hours. Partway through their marathon of math, Chrissy went to the kitchen to make them some hot cocoa. Todd wandered around her living room, realizing he had never been up here before. He surveyed her bookshelves, surprised to see rows of books full of travel guides and non-fiction books about countries all over the world. *I wonder what that is about.* As far as he knew, Chrissy had never been anywhere except the short time she was off at college. She never talked about going anywhere, or even *wanting* to go somewhere.

Chrissy came back with the cocoa, and he vocalized his curiosity. He gestured to the travel books. "Have you gone to any of these places?"

Chrissy shifted her weight and shook her head adamantly. "Nah, I don't actually want to go anywhere. I just love to read about different places." Then, she changed the subject.

Todd decided not to push and they went back to their work. Looking at one inventory item after another, until both of them could barely keep their eyes open. It was after midnight.

Pulling her ponytail loose and running a hand through her hair. The scent of her shampoo filled the small space between them on the couch. "Todd, I don't know how to thank you. I don't know how you learned to do all this." She paused and considered. "Actually, how *did* you learn to do all this?" Chrissy eyed him with one raised eyebrow. "You are super good with the spreadsheet and everything."

Todd looked away, shifting his weight on the couch. "I don't know, I guess I just kind of picked it up along the way, running my own business and all." He rubbed his beard.

"I don't believe you." Todd was hiding something, and Chrissy was bound and determined to get it out.

Todd rubbed a hand back and forth across the back of his neck. "Ah geez. I guess I better just tell you." He paused, and Chrissy nearly vibrated in the silence.

"Well?!"

Todd exhaled a breath, and his confession with it. "I've been going to school for the last two years."

Chrissy flinched. "You what?"

"I have one more semester left and I'll have my degree in business and construction management."

Chrissy was shaking her head in silence. "I can't believe you have been doing this for *two freaking years* and you never told me. Does everyone know? Does Luke know?" Chrissy was ticked. Beyond ticked. Todd had never seen her like this, even when Bobby Kratz had stolen her journal from her locker and started reading portions of it out loud to the lunch table.

"Chrissy, it's not like that. Nobody knows. You are the first person I've told." Todd pleaded with her. He needed her to understand.

Chrissy stood up and paced. "I can't believe

you've been lying this whole time, Todd. Why would you do that? Did you think we wouldn't support you? I thought we were friends."

"Chrissy, listen – " Todd stood and took a step toward the woman he loved.

"I think you need to leave." Chrissy crossed her arms and turned toward her bookshelves.

Todd reached a hand toward her, imploring her to listen. "Just let me – "

"Get. Out."

His hand dropped to his side and he hung his head. Todd spoke to her back, into the angry silence. "I'm sorry, Chris." Then, when she didn't respond with so much as a wave, he gathered his coat and left.

*a*fter Todd left her loft, Chrissy paced the small space trying to process what he told her. His confession about attending college felt like getting kicked in the stomach. They had been friends since she was eight years old and discovered Todd lived a few houses down. Chrissy never cared that Todd wasn't the smartest boy in class. He always made her feel special, just like he had earlier— holding her and telling her how much he believed in her. She recalled the kiss in front of the nativity, and the ones last night at the cafe.

Todd was important to her.

Clearly, he didn't feel the same way about her.

If he did, he wouldn't have been able to lie to her for so long. How could he kiss her while he was lying to her the whole time? Her own unwelcome thought came then, *you haven't exactly been honest with him, either.* Chrissy considered that fact and quickly justified her omission. Todd's secret was something good, something he should have been willing to share. Her secret was awful and dark and shameful. Besides, Chrissy's secret was in the past and Todd's? He was lying every single day. When he skipped out on plans or had to leave early, it was all because he was in school. Chrissy tried to understand what could have possessed him to hide something so big from his closest friends but couldn't.

She stopped pacing and considered Todd again, adding this new information to the file. She thought about how she had always viewed Todd, through the lens of his nearly dropping out of school. Todd was the boy who never raised his hand to offer an answer during school. Presumably because he never knew the answer. Chrissy had never seen him with a book, never even seen him use a computer. She remembered the 3-D renditions he had done for her café. It was impossible to reconcile the man who created those and a man she didn't think knew what a computer spreadsheet was. Chrissy was so caught up in the excitement of the renovation that she hadn't even made the connection at first.

She was becoming increasingly comfortable with the unexpected feeling of romance in their old, familiar friendship before the secret came out, which made it hurt even more. Between waiting tables and trying to catch time with her Dad to learn about the business of the cafe, thoughts of what a relationship with Todd would mean had consumed every spare minute. And they were such positive thoughts! But now? All those ideas and dreams were tainted with frustration and tears at the sense of betrayal. Crying, she practically stomped from couch to bookshelf to kitchen to couch again. She spent too long in an exhausted state trying to understand. She alternated between thoughts that intensified and extinguished her anger, before falling into a dreamless sleep on the sofa. Two empty hot cocoa mugs still sat on the coffee table in front of her.

TODD WALKED to his car slowly, reliving the hurt and anger on Chrissy's face over and over again. She was right, he had lied to her, but if she would just let him explain. If she would just let him reassure her that he was going to tell her, eventually. The hardest part was Todd was finally being honest, after lying for years. Not just for the two years he'd been in school; he'd actually been lying all the years before that.

He had lied since he was a little kid and his father had made fun of him for coming home from school and talking excitedly about the book they were reading in class. He lied after his father had taken away all his books when he was seven years old, saying they were making Todd 'a sissy boy'. That pain—the pain of having his interests and favorite activities mocked—had destroyed him. Todd stopped reading; he stopped participating in class. Instead, he played sports and made jokes and tried to be the son his father wanted.

But inside, he was longing to learn.

Hiding books under his bed. Completing his homework and then never handing it in. Todd was finally being honest and doing something worthwhile. Finally looking forward, albeit nervously, to showing his friends this side of him. But, would they still be his friends? The Todd they knew was a lie. Maybe they wouldn't like the new Todd—the *real* Todd.

It was late and bitter cold, but Todd didn't even feel it. So intense was the worry and regret he felt— he never meant to hurt Chrissy. In fact, he was extremely grateful he had the skills to help her tackle this unexpected new challenge in her life. His only option now was to pray she would forgive him. Maybe Chrissy would come to see him as he'd always wanted her to: intelligent, hardworking, and good enough. Because when he was in high school, scraping by when he knew he could have done so much more, the hardest part was watching Chrissy stand up next to the other high-achievers. Sitting there in the audience, wanting desperately to be good enough for her, but knowing she deserved to be with someone like the guys standing up there with her.

Could he be that guy now? Todd was starting to think so. Soon, he would have the degree. And if his business continued to grow, he would be able to show the world—and Chrissy—he was more than the dumb-jock he'd always portrayed. He wasn't giving up on her. Or his dreams. His thoughts circled back to the hurt look on Christine's face when he revealed his secret. He hoped she could forgive him eventually. Surely, she wouldn't hold a grudge for long.

After arriving home, still worrying and wondering how to approach his next conversation with Chrissy, he started measuring and cutting wood for the first of fifteen tables. It was nearly two in the morning, but he wouldn't be able to sleep. Todd needed to pour his frustration into something and wood had always been a willing vessel. More than most projects, Todd poured his heart and soul into the wood for this table. With each saw cut, each screw, and each stroke of the sander; he thought of Chrissy and their relationship. His understanding of the phrase 'blood, sweat, and tears' took on a whole new meaning, more than one tear escaping as he relived their growing closeness over the last few weeks and contemplated the possibility of losing Chrissy forever.

CHRISSY NEEDED to talk to someone, but with every name she considered—she realized spilling Todd's secret wasn't something she could do. Which ruled out everyone she could think of. Mandy, Charlotte. All of them knew Todd and would know who she spoke about. In the end, Chrissy called her mom and tried not to be too obvious. Janine desperately wanted her daughter to settle down and start having grandbabies with "a nice young man".

It was hard to share without giving away the

details, but Chrissy tried to explain. "I've been sort of falling for this guy."

"Oh Chrissy, that's wonderful! What's his name?" Janine's voice rose an entire octave and Chrissy pulled the phone away from her ear.

"Mom, just wait. We've just been hanging out. Nothing too serious. I really like him, but it turns out he has been lying to me the whole time. I don't know what to do about it." Chrissy cringed. This was a disaster.

Her mom was sufficiently sympathetic, but she didn't outright condemn the mystery man like Chrissy kind of hoped.

Janine probed gently, "Did he apologize? Do you believe him?"

Chrissy admitted the truth. "I didn't exactly give him a chance to apologize." She shook her head. "I just don't understand why he would lie about it in the first place."

Janine gave a non-committal noise. "Well, everyone makes mistakes sweetie. Did you ask him why he lied?"

Chrissy recalled their conversation. "No, I don't suppose I did. I kind of kicked him out as soon as the truth came out."

"If you think you could really love him, he must

be a good guy and he probably deserves the chance to explain." Janine hesitated, unsure of whether to continue. "Christine, this is the first time I've heard you talk about liking someone since before college, sweetie. Since..." She trailed off, leaving the events unspoken. But Chrissy knew what her mom was talking about. Since the night in Chicago. "That's a big deal. Don't throw it away over something that you might be able to forgive."

Chrissy considered that. Could she forgive Todd for lying? Maybe. But there were more implications of this revelation. She'd always viewed Todd as a hard-working, handsome, funny man with a solid faith. But she had always taken pride in the fact that she had done well in high school and gone to college. She hadn't finished, but Todd had never even gone. In some ways, she'd always felt like her intelligence and accomplishments evened the playing field between them a bit.

But now? She was a too-curvy college dropout who'd been damaged—possibly beyond repair. And Todd? Todd was not only hard-working, handsome, and funny—he was smart and would have a degree to help him run his own successful business. The only reason she had a business at all was because her parents gave it to her. She hadn't earned anything, and the whole process of taking over the cafe had really revealed that she wasn't as smart or capable as she'd once thought.

Todd deserved better.

And Chrissy either needed to find someone back on her level, or become content in her singleness. Didn't Paul say singleness was a gift in the New Testament? Never having another night like the one they spent hanging up decorations didn't sound like a gift to her. And the thought of never having someone to kiss under the mistletoe made her chest ache.

There was too much Todd didn't know about her. And while she definitely couldn't come out and tell him Chicago, she could do the unselfish thing and let him go. He would find someone else. Chrissy knew he hadn't dated anyone since high school but once she made it clear she wasn't interested, he would move on. He had to. She would just put him firmly back in the 'friend' category where he'd been for so long.

11

*I*t was mid-December now, and Chrissy knew she only had a couple of weeks before her parents left. She resolved to keep Todd firmly in the friend-zone and threw herself into the long list of things that needed to be done before they left. She met with Charlotte and interviewed the candidates from Craigslist and others that Charlotte had found from an online job board. Some of the candidates were laughable and had apparently considered manning the grill at McDonald's as enough experience to run a kitchen as chef. A couple candidates were more promising though. Charlotte was amazing and sat in every interview, taking notes. She let Chrissy lead the interviews though, only speaking up to ask a follow-up question or two.

After the interviews, Charlotte talked to Chrissy about what she saw and heard, many were things Chrissy never even picked up on. "I get the feeling this guy was actually more of a kitchen assistant for this restaurant in Indianapolis. He never said anything about making decisions or creating dishes."

By their final interview, Chrissy was more confident about her ability to interview the candidates and had narrowed the list down to three people. She and Charlotte sat at a booth in the cafe, drinking a cup of coffee and debriefing about the last interview, discussing the next steps.

"I think the next step is to taste their food, right?" Chrissy looked to Charlotte for confirmation.

Charlotte laughed. "That makes sense to me, but I've never hired a cook before! Do you want them to cook something of their choice or something you assign to them?"

Chrissy thought about it. "Hmmm. I'd actually like them to do both. I want to see how creative they are, but also how well they can make something unfamiliar. I'm still working on the menu. Ideally, we would create the menu together." Chrissy had her own ideas for food and she did like to cook, but she thought the right cook would be able to complement her style and give B&J Bistro a unique flair. Plus, the cook would probably think of aspects of the kitchen and menu that Chrissy might not consider.

"Sounds like a great idea. Just one more thing," Charlotte said excitedly. "I want to help judge the dishes. It will be my favorite interview yet, I'm sure!"

Chrissy grinned and nodded. Charlotte had never been shy about her love of food. "I'd love to have you there for a second opinion. I'm thinking I'll have them each make fried chicken with sides and then a dish of their choice. No matter what the bistro menu features, we will have to have some of the homestyle classics on it, too." Her current regulars were mostly a down-home cooking kind of crowd. They had a salad at the cafe now, but Chrissy was pretty sure the only person who had ever ordered it was currently sitting across from her. It was going to be a delicate balance to create a menu that would satisfy the expectations of the old farmers who'd been coming to Bud and Janine's since it opened, and also try to draw in new clientele.

"Sounds yummy. I think you should call the finalists and explain what you want from them. They already know about your plans to transition to a more sophisticated menu after the grand re-opening in February. On each call you can make it clear that you want their chef's choice meal to be something bistro-worthy."

Chrissy agreed. "Okay. I suppose I'll have to call the others and tell them they didn't get the job." She frowned at the prospect of delivering the bad news.

Charlotte laughed. "Yes, unfortunately, that's a part of the process. Telling someone they didn't get the job isn't nearly as bad as telling someone they are fired, though!"

Chrissy remembered a few waitresses being fired by her parents over the years for skipping out on shifts and, in one case, stealing. "Oh great, something else I probably have to look forward to someday."

"Hopefully not for a long time. And if you do a good job hiring upfront, it makes it a lot less likely."

Chrissy had to agree and she was flooded with gratitude for all the help Charlotte had given her so far. Chrissy had only known Charlotte for a few months, but they had quickly become great friends. "I'm so glad you are here to help with that part." Charlotte's expertise in reading people and interviewing had been a godsend. One less thing for Chrissy to struggle through on her own. Her parents were almost gone and she'd been pushing Todd away with each of his visits to the cafe.

TODD TRIED to have lunch at the cafe a couple of times after their fight. Chrissy was nice but not warm and friendly in her usual way. She was still angry with him, unable to answer her own questions about their future. Instead of the man she was kissing under the mistletoe only a week ago, she treated Todd like an old acquaintance. The more Todd tried to interject and explain or bring up the fight, the harder Chrissy worked to avoid the conversations— ducking into the kitchen and having extended conversations with other patrons.

It was driving him crazy, so Todd did the only thing he knew to do. He worked and he prayed. Todd built table after table, getting more efficient with each completion. Finals were coming up in less than a week, so he studied and worked some more. He didn't stop going to the cafe, though. Even if it took until Christmas next year, he knew he could wear Chrissy down. Todd wasn't going to let her go. Since they were eight years old, he'd known she was special. And since she came back to Minden after college, he saw her nearly every day, and considered her one of his best friends. The only thing keeping him from pursuing her sooner was his fear of inadequacy. With his finished degree close enough to taste, Todd vowed he wouldn't let her go again. When she had gone away to Chicago, he was sure she would never come back.

Todd loved Minden and this little corner of Indiana they'd carved out. But a lot of folks didn't. It was hard to resist the allure of the city; the restaurants, concerts, and sporting events. He'd never been a big fan of loud music and while Todd loved a good baseball game as much as the next guy—he'd never been comfortable in a crowd that size. Plus, paying ten bucks for a beer seemed like highway robbery. As much as he loved Minden, he knew if it meant having Chrissy, he'd gladly move to the heart of downtown and enjoy every second of it. Luckily, she came back to town. And now that the cafe was hers, she wouldn't want to leave again. At least, he hoped that was the case.

Todd was dreading Christmas, now only a couple weeks away. Being upset about Chrissy shouldn't ruin the entire holiday for him, but somehow it seemed like it would. He even took the long way when he needed to go through town so he wouldn't have to see the Christmas tree or the

Nativity scene. The Nativity only reminded his pride at telling Chrissy he made it and would be making her tables. And the kiss that had followed there in the cold. And then, later that night and revealing to her that he'd been lying about who he was.

When Sunday came around, Todd was glad for the chance to see his friends and to experience the worship and fellowship he always reveled in. He'd skipped the first Sunday after the fight, thinking he would give Chrissy space and instead had stayed home and watched a sermon online. It hadn't done much to refresh his spirit though. Todd hadn't even reached out to his best friends, Luke or Mark, about the situation. Mainly because he was lying to them, too. As much as he wanted to tell them everything about Chrissy and their kiss—and then the fight—it would mean telling them his secret. He wasn't ready for that either.

Instead, he kept to himself and oscillated between feelings of guilt and resolve, anger and self-pity. Over the last two years, Todd had rationalized the lies of omission to his closest friends. He even felt pretty close to God during that time. But now, he had seen the hurt in Chrissy's eyes and really thought about the times he'd made excuses or avoided his friends because of the truth. He realized it was a glaring sin he'd ignored too long.

Todd recalled the verse in Matthew, one he'd always noticed with his carpentry background. "Why do you look at the speck of sawdust in your brother's eye and pay no attention to the plank in your own eye?" For more than two years, Todd had counseled friends on struggles in their lives, but paid no attention to the giant two-by-four smack in the middle of his own. And now, his lack of honesty could cost him the woman of his dreams. He didn't want it to cost him his friendships too. Todd had to come clean to Luke and Mark. He wanted to tell Miss Ruth himself, too. She had always been like a mother to him. *Maybe Ruth would be the easiest to tell. I can't see her not forgiving easily.*

His mind made up, Todd tried to refocus on the church service happening around him. He joined the final hymn with a lighter heart than he'd had all week. The decision to let the truth be known was a weight lifted off his chest he hadn't even realized he was carrying. He found Luke after the service and asked if he had time to meet up later. Miss Ruth was as gracious and warm as ever as she gave him a quick hug in the church foyer as they were leaving.

"I'll see you this afternoon, honey."

Luke wasn't free until late afternoon, so Todd spent the a few hours working and praying. Unlike the last week though, his prayers weren't filled with pleas for forgiveness by Chrissy, or prayers for patience through her stubbornness. These prayers were filled with repentance and confession. They were deep and healing and cathartic in a way that Todd hadn't known since his first prayers as a new Christian. This lie had wormed its way into his life and he was struck with the realization of why he allowed it.

I'm so sorry God. I let my lie invade my life. And even though I was spending time with you, there was something in the way, wasn't there? Because it was unresolved. I let my pride guide my actions, instead of my faith in you. You are so good, Father. I never want to let a secret impact my testimony.

Why did you?

Deep in prayer, Todd felt the question asked silently, deep in his spirit. *I still believed that I wasn't good enough. That people wouldn't love the real me. Somehow, I thought I couldn't let them see me. But I know you created me and that you love me with a perfect love. That the approval of this world doesn't matter, God. But the approval of my friends? Doesn't it matter?*

You are my workmanship.

Todd soaked in the verse and continued its prompt. *I am your workmanship, created in Christ Jesus for good works, which You prepared in advance for me to do. I want to do Your works, Father. I am Your workmanship. I won't be ashamed of who I am any longer. My earthly father is not a reflection of You, my heavenly Father.*

Later that afternoon, Todd met with Ruth, sitting down for a long chat. Ruth was patient, never rushing him. She poured him lemonade and stacked a few cookies on his plate as they sat at her cozy kitchen table. She chatted about the upcoming wedding and asked him about his business. Swallowing a bite of cookie, Todd took his opening and told her everything. He told her how business was taking off, and about how he'd been dishonest the last several years. She tilted her head in confusion and he revealed that he would graduate in May from college. Before he'd even finished, Ruth was up and hugging him with a huge smile on her face.

"Oh, I'm so proud of you, Todd Flynn. I always knew you had it in you. I can't believe you kept it a secret for so long, but I'm so glad you've told me now." She patted his cheek. "You've always been far smarter than folks gave you credit for, something you never bothered to correct them on." She shook her head and sat back down. "Heaven knows why you let people think you were anything less than you are. Oh, child. Good for you!" She continued to praise him and reaffirm his abilities as they finished their lemonade. She waved away his apologies for the dishonesty and assured him, "The only thing that matters is that you are being honest now."

Ruth sent him on his way to tell Luke, with promises to send him study snacks for the following week of finals. "I always sent care packages to my Rachel during finals. It takes a lot of energy to work your mind that hard in one week."

Luke was more difficult to tell, but he didn't take it hard. Sometimes Todd forgot that Luke hadn't known him in high school. Luke came back from college with Ruth's daughter, Rachel, one Thanksgiving and never left. Todd didn't have to change Luke's perception as much as he had to explain the dishonesty.

Luke knew about his father—they'd discussed it before—but Todd did explain a little of the 'why' behind his decision to keep it from his friends.

"To please my dad, I never read books or put forth any effort except in sports. Everybody sees me as a dumb jock, Luke." Todd hung his head. "I didn't want to hear people saying that I was wasting my time trying to go to college. And I didn't know if people would still want to be my friend if I wasn't the guy they thought I'd always been." Todd shrugged as though it were no big deal to reveal his deepest insecurity out loud. Those thoughts of doubt and fear were the ones he had never really verbalized until now.

"I guess I get it. My mom wasn't exactly a shining example of God's love. But let me tell you something." Luke looked him straight in the eye. "If you think people only see you as a dumb jock, you couldn't be more wrong. This community has seen you the past decade since high school. No matter who you pretended to be back then—you haven't really been that guy since. In Minden, you are a talented construction worker, an outstanding man, and a role model to the high school guys at church."

Luke shook his head and continued, "Todd, you are giving and hardworking and—except for this admittedly big secret—honest. Since your dad died, the only person convinced you are anything less than awesome is you."

The words sounded similar to what Mark had told him a few weeks ago. Todd said a quick prayer of thanks for the godly counsel of the friends in his life.

Their forgiveness and encouragement was exactly the reassurance he needed to push forward with Chrissy. There was no question he'd messed up, but he would do everything he could to make it up to her and get her to trust him again.

12

---

*A*t church that morning, Chrissy stubbornly avoided looking at Todd and barely heard the sermon. She was too busy planning her week ahead. It was easier to focus on the restaurant than on the friend she was angry with. The first of her potential new cooks would be auditioning tonight, with the others to follow on Monday and Tuesday. Her parents moving date was next weekend, a little more than a week before Christmas. When they'd first announced the moving date, she hadn't really registered that it meant she would be spending Christmas alone. They'd do Christmas as a family next weekend, but Chrissy knew it wouldn't be the same. Instead of focusing on the holiday she was now dreading, she worked on the menu ideas for the bistro.

By the time Charlotte arrived for the interview, Chrissy was making good progress with the menu. She forgot about Todd and his lies for the afternoon. The candidate cooking tonight was named Lauren. From their first interview, Chrissy remembered that she worked as a cook at a chain restaurant in Terre Haute. Chrissy had gotten the ingredients the cook had requested and laid them out in the kitchen. She planned to hang out near the kitchen, available in case Lauren needed help finding anything, but also to observe how composed she remained while cooking the two meals. Lauren had requested a variety of ingredients and appeared to be making a pasta dish. Carbs were never a bad idea and Chrissy was looking forward to tasting it.

When Lauren arrived, Chrissy showed her the kitchen and told her to help herself to whatever she needed in order to complete the meals. Each time Chrissy peeked in to the kitchen, she saw Lauren contentedly stirring a pot, chopping something or standing at the fryer. It looked like it was going well.

When Lauren brought out two plates of her pasta dish, Chrissy thought it looked okay. It wasn't beautiful, but what could she expect from pasta with a red sauce? Lauren brought out the fried chicken immediately after.

Unfortunately, as comfortable as Lauren appeared to be in the kitchen, it was clear she was not the cook for the bistro. The noodles were still crunchy and the sauce tasted like the can of diced tomatoes Chrissy had supplied per instructions. Crispy, golden skin of the chicken disguised the still raw meat on the inside—forcing Chrissy and Charlotte to spit it out. The green beans were dumped from a can and the mashed potatoes were gummy, as though they had been processed in the blender.

After a few incredulous glances and very few words exchanged, Chrissy went to find Lauren in the kitchen. She was sitting on one of the barstools browsing her phone. That one behavior made her realize how young Lauren looked, only in her very early twenties. Chrissy eyed the mess in the kitchen with resignation, knowing that she'd end up cleaning it tonight.

Chrissy got her attention. "Hey Lauren, I want you to come taste your food as well."

Back at the table, she slid a plate to Lauren and let her taste the pasta.

Lauren frowned and spit out the bite in a napkin. "What's wrong with it? I mean, why isn't it cooked all the way? I cooked it just like I did at Italian Family. And this sauce you bought is terrible."

Chrissy raised her eyebrows. "Lauren, I didn't buy sauce. I bought *ingredients*. You said to buy 'Italian Diced Tomatoes' and that's what I got."

"Well, the bag we used at Italian Family was called Tuscan Diced Tomato and made our famous Tuscan Rustic Tomato Pasta. All we had to do was heat it up and serve over pasta. And the pasta only took, like five minutes in the water to be done." Lauren's valley-girl inflection and innocent, wide eyes and made Chrissy want to roll her own.

It all started to make sense to Chrissy. Lauren may have 'cooked' at the restaurant, but she couldn't cook. Her experience was limited to opening packages and heating pre-seasoned sauces. "Those noodles must have been par-boiled." At Lauren's confused face, Chrissy explained. "It means that it was partially cooked before you cooked it. Like instant rice compared to regular rice." Chrissy waved a hand, not willing to expand further. "Look, I really appreciate you coming in for this second interview, but I think we need someone with more experience cooking from scratch."

"But what about the chicken? I even looked that up on the internet while I was in the kitchen because

I'd never made it. I didn't know it would be, like, raw when I got here!" Lauren sounded defensive, unwilling to admit defeat.

Irritated at the immature girl, Chrissy tried to be patient and showed her the still-raw interior. "I think you missed something. It takes at least ten minutes in the fryer to cook fried chicken."

"Well, I mean, I saw that in the recipe. But I just turned up the dial on the fryer a little bit and cut the time. Shorter ticket times are good for the kitchen, right? I didn't want to burn it, so I just took it out when it looked done."

After briefly explaining that you couldn't cook chicken all the way through without enough time, Chrissy finally managed to send Lauren out the door with best wishes. She sat down next to Charlotte and sighed. She playfully smacked her head on the counter a couple of times. "I'm doomed, Charlotte."

Charlotte just started laughing and Chrissy soon joined in. "Oh my goodness. Can you imagine just dumping out a can of diced tomatoes and thinking that would taste good over pasta? It's so watery." Charlotte lifted a forkful of the pasta dish and watched the pink juice drip back into the plate.

"Thanks for coming tonight. Can I make you some real food?" Chrissy offered as she walked back into the kitchen. She stopped short just inside the door and Charlotte soon bumped into her backside. Chrissy sighed again, studying the mess. There was a pot still bubbling and spattering sauce on the stove, flour covering the counter, the raw chicken wrapper cast to one side without a care for the unsanitary condition it created. Empty cans and plastic wrappers littered the countertop and floor. It looked as though fifty dinners had been made in the kitchen with no time to clean, instead of two meals with no time limit.

Charlotte gave her a friendly smile and went to the fridge. "How about I make us both a sandwich while you get this kitchen back to the spotless refuge you love so much?"

That was an offer Chrissy couldn't refuse, and she nodded gratefully. "Thanks, hon. You're the best."

THE CANDIDATE on Monday night was better, but still not what Chrissy needed. Emma was about Chrissy's age, maybe slightly older and was very stoic and professional during the interview. She had at least managed to get the chicken cooked through, but her signature recipe for the bistro menu was nothing special. While Chrissy thought quiche had potential for a brunch menu or special, this one wasn't great. The crust was dry, the filling under seasoned. And the chosen flavors? Chrissy didn't think tofu, mushroom, and kale was going to appeal to her clientele. Even Charlotte, with her city background and penchant for yoga and hippie-dippy food, wasn't on board with the selection.

But Emma could at least function independently in the kitchen, so Chrissy didn't cut her loose entirely, figuring Emma was probably trainable as a last resort. As she cleaned up the kitchen from another cook's mess, she prayed for God to send her the right partner for the bistro.

That prayer was repeated without ceasing until Tuesday night. The last candidate was named Norman. She'd scheduled him last, with high hopes. According to his resume and interview, Norm had worked for a several locally-owned restaurants in Chicago and Indianapolis. She remembered wondering why on earth he would want to work in Minden, and Charlotte had asked him that same question point-blank.

Norm explained he grew up nearby and needed to move back to the area to be closer to his parents as they got older. He was probably close to fifty himself, and like any good cook—in her mind, anyway—carried a bit of extra weight around his middle. His thick mustache was beginning to have more salt than pepper, much like the rest of his thick hair. Frankly, Norm brought a ton of experience to the table if he could back up his resume with actual food.

Norm showed up right on time and got to work after a quick tour of the kitchen. He popped out to ask Chrissy a question or two while cooking, but mostly she and Charlotte sat at the counter and talked while listening to him mutter to himself, and occasionally sing, as he cooked for them. When he placed the first plates in the window and rang the bell with a well-practiced "Order Up!" Chrissy felt a thrill. It felt right. Now, she just had to see how the food tasted.

Norman had started with the fried chicken. Everything on the plate was hot and well-seasoned. Charlotte took a bite of the mashed potatoes and groaned. "These are the best mashed potatoes I've ever had, Chris."

Chrissy had to agree. No shortcuts here. Clumps of real potatoes meant they weren't instant. Chrissy had no doubt it was real butter and real sour cream that made them taste so good. The chicken was equally impressive. Crispy and juicy, salty and full of flavor. She desperately wondered how he had done it so quickly. Before she had time to wonder too long, she heard the familiar bell and another "Order Up!"

Chrissy retrieved the plates from the window and was pleased to see a delicious looking sandwich artfully arranged on an unfamiliar plate. It was paired with sweet potato fries and a small bowl of fresh fruit. As she and Charlotte admired the plates, she called for Norman to come out.

He wiped his hands with a dish towel and she smiled warmly. "Would you tell us about what you've made?"

"Absolutely, ladies." Norm came over to the counter. "This is a hot turkey caprese sandwich on sourdough. It features a homemade garlic-basil aioli, fresh tomatoes, and mozzarella cheese. On the side are sweet potato fries served with a creamy maple dipping sauce and fruit."

After he confirmed they didn't have any questions, Norm went back in the kitchen. The food was delicious. Chrissy loved the sandwich and the way the homemade mayo sauce made it seem like so much more than turkey on bread. The fries were crispy and the maple sauce wasn't overly sweet. She also loved that Norman had cared enough about the presentation to bring his own long, rectangular plates which gave the entire dish an upscale feel.

"I think I've got a cook." She looked at Charlotte, only to find her with her mouth full and eyes closed; savoring her last bite of the sandwich. She laughed at the embarrassed look on Charlotte's face and waited for her to speak.

"No, I think you've got a chef."

Chrissy nodded in agreement and went to the kitchen to give Norman the good news. Her heart soared when she found him wiping down the countertops while the dishes he used ran in the industrial dishwasher, which hummed in the background. Words tumbled out before she could stop them. "You're an angel, Norman."

He laughed and replied, "Hardly. But a good chef always leaves behind a clean kitchen."

"No seriously, Norman, you are an absolute answer to prayer. I would love it if you would be the next chef for Bud and Janine's Cafe, and eventually for B&J's Bistro."

After insisting she call him Norm, and a review of the cafe hours, he accepted and agreed to start the following Sunday, working side-by-side with Chrissy in the kitchen for the first couple of days until he learned the recipes and lay of the land.

"I do have to ask you one more thing. How did you make fried chicken so good in so little time?"

Norm laughed. "Well, you told me I'd be making fried chicken. So, I started some chicken soaking in buttermilk yesterday morning and brought it with me. I figured it's what I would do if I was cooking here, so it was fair game. Any fried chicken worth eating needs plenty of time soaking to make sure it is nice and juicy."

"Well, it paid off. It was some of the best fried chicken I've ever had." Then, she added with a guilty smile, "But don't tell my dad that."

13

*C*hrissy was living with a constant headache and almost no sleep. Every night, she tossed and turned, running through endless to-do lists and dreaming about her future as a business owner. She was running on coffee alone. She woke up with a sore throat and absolutely no time to be sick, but Chrissy switched to tea with honey and powered through the fatigue. The more time she spent making decisions and putting her stamp on the bistro, the more she loved the challenge. She found herself with renewed mental energy, despite the increased stress levels. It had been years since she really tackled a problem head-on. Unknowingly, she had let 'safe' in Minden mean boring and low-responsibility.

It was the complete opposite of her natural achiever mentality. The cafe was hers now, and she was going to make it the best restaurant in Indiana— or at least in the county. Unfortunately, that determination means she was the only one working until Norm was trained. Her dad was still there a few hours a day, but mostly he was getting things squared away at the house. If she didn't do something, it didn't get done—and that wasn't an option.

Mandy came into the cafe and took one look at Chrissy. She blurted out with her usual lack of finesse, "You look awful."

After collapsing into the nearest barstool, Chrissy dropped her head into her hands and moaned. "I feel awful."

Mandy removed her scarf and coat and dropped her things into the chair of a nearby table before approaching Chrissy's spot at the counter. She rubbed her back and waited until Chrissy looked up at her. This time, Mandy spoke softly. "You need to go to the doctor, Chrissy."

Chrissy shook her head. "I can't. I haven't been to a doctor in years. I don't even have a doctor!"

Mandy gave an unsympathetic look. "Then find one. You haven't been taking care of yourself and pretty soon you are going to faint in the middle of the cafe. Probably holding a tray with five plates on it." Then, she added with a grimace, "Plus, no one wants a sick waitress."

"I know, I know." Chrissy looked up at Mandy. "Where do you go to the doctor?"

"There's a family medicine clinic over in Green-castle that I go to." Greencastle was a larger town about fifteen minutes away, and home to the closest actual grocery store. "They've got a couple doctors and I can usually get an appointment pretty easily. I think they just got a new doctor, too, so they probably have openings for new patients."

"Fine. I'll go." She wiped her nose and a cough racked her body. "Anything is better than feeling like this." Chrissy gathered her strength and lifted her head from its place on the counter. "What can I get for you?"

Mandy laughed. "You just stay right there and don't worry about me." She walked behind the counter and retrieved a ceramic mug from the shelf and poured herself a cup of coffee. She also got a mug of hot water and a teabag, added a spoonful of honey and brought both mugs to the counter. Then she served herself a piece of French silk pie from the bakery case and sat back down next to Chrissy. "So, tell me what's got you so worn out? I hope it's late nights watching movies with Todd."

THE IMPROMPTU THERAPY session with Mandy was surprisingly helpful for Chrissy. She bemoaned her parents' sudden departure and the stress of trying to run a business by herself. She mentioned that she and Todd were fighting. Todd had admitted his secret schooling to everyone at that point, so Mandy and Chrissy talked about it at length. In the end, despite Mandy's straightforward opinion that Chrissy should "Get over it and forgive the poor guy," Chrissy was still unable to do so.

When she prayed about it, she felt the push to forgive Todd. He'd apologized and come clean to every one. Admittedly, she'd moved past the anger, but the betrayal still stung. Maybe it was possible for her and Todd to be friends again. No more than that, though.

Mandy also gave Chrissy a lot of encouragement on the business front. After all, Mandy ran her own business, too. The daycare might not have been the same as a restaurant, but Mandy understood the stress of being the CEO—Chief Everything Officer, as she called it—and having the entire thing rest on your shoulders. Before Mandy left, she made Chrissy call and schedule an appointment with the doctor for the next day. Chrissy hated doing it, but she hung a "Closed" sign on the cafe at two o'clock the next day.

She drove to Greencastle and filled out the new patient paperwork for the clinic while sitting in the unremarkable waiting room. After waiting, the nurse called her back and she was measured and weighed in the hallway. Despite the temptation to close her eyes as the numbers on the scale were displayed, she looked and then winced. Her mother's voice in her head lamented the extra rolls she had eaten on Thanksgiving and she stepped off the scale. When Chrissy met the doctor, she was immediately aware of how young and attractive he was. He didn't seem to be much older than thirty and he was slim and fit, with the build of a runner. Neatly trimmed hair and a clean-shaven face contributed to his youthful appearance.

Chrissy's perusal of the new doctor was interrupted as he held out his hand to shake hers. "Hi, I'm Dr. Pike. What brings you in today?"

Chrissy explained the sore throat and fatigue and the sinus headache she seemed to have acquired in the last few days. Dr. Pike nodded and waited for her to continue. Before she could stop it, she dumped all her stress and worries in a giant word pile in the exam room. He was a good listener, and when she finally ran out of words, her face flushed in embarrassment. Doctors didn't want to hear every detail! She tried to apologize but her waved her off with a polite smile. Then, he listened to her take a few deep breaths and checked her throat and ears with the little flashlight before he spoke.

"Well, Chrissy, I think you've got a run-of-the-mill cold. It's a virus, so there isn't much I can do for you. But I think it is being made much worse by the stress you are under. You need to slow down and take some time to rest and recover. Or you risk your cold turning into bronchitis or pneumonia." The lecture was given in a stern but gentle voice. "Sounds like you've been having trouble sleeping?" Chrissy nodded. "Along with your official prescription of slowing down, lots of fluids, and some over the counter cold medicine, I'm going to give you a couple of doses of a sleep aid. It should help you calm down and not be so anxious at night. If you don't get better in a week or so, come back and see me and we will reevaluate." He was writing a note as he spoke. "Where do you want your prescription sent?"

After saying she would pick it up at the one-hour pharmacy there in Greencastle, Chrissy was free to go. She was thankful she didn't have to work tonight. Maybe she'd take one of those sleeping pills this afternoon and try to squeeze some extra rest before Sunday, when Norm was due to come in for training. As she wandered through the pharmacy, picking up cough drops, cold medicine, extra Kleenexes, and emergency chocolate, she thought about the charming doctor.

Chrissy hadn't seen a ring on his finger, and he had been very handsome—if a girl was into the lean athletic type. She compared it to the muscular football-player build she preferred, but was frustrated when the face attached to the muscular body she pictured was none other than Todd. Did she prefer the muscular body-type? Or did she just prefer Todd? Whatever the reason, she knew the doctor didn't do anything for her, despite his obvious good qualities. *Not that he'd go for me anyway... A runner and a chocoholic? No chance.* Chrissy grabbed another bag of Dark Chocolate Caramels with Sea Salt for good measure and headed back to the pharmacy.

14

While Chrissy was busy interviewing for the cook and fighting a stress-induced cold, Todd was spending every spare moment studying and taking his finals. He used Chrissy's renovation as the capstone for his Project Management class. He created a timeline for the project and submitted the 3-D renderings of the space. At the last minute, Todd realized he was missing the budget he needed to submit as part of the assignment.

Todd pulled out his laptop to work up the quote. He'd already ordered the reclaimed wood and the tile they had chosen together. He added a line item for labor, resolving to finish the quote like it was any other customer before trying to work some magic for

Chrissy. Todd added materials and labor rates for counters, painting, and everything associated with replacing the light fixtures. As the numbers added up in the bottom right of the spreadsheet, his heart sank. He should have done this weeks ago, when they first discussed the scope of the renovation. The worked-up budget and the rest of the project documents were due at midnight, but he got it done just in time.

Now, he needed to talk to Chrissy. Many of the tables were already complete but Todd had never given Chrissy an estimate for the furniture and renovations.

With their relationship so strained, he knew it was a bad time, but she needed to know what she was getting into. Todd had no idea if she had the money to take on the renovations, and they hadn't spoken any further about the loan. It was foolish to have put up money for the materials before they had everything finalized. If it turned out she couldn't afford it, it would be heart breaking. Todd would do anything to make it happen for her, even if it meant taking next to nothing for his time and labor on the project. *Not exactly a savvy business decision, Todd.* He wasn't thinking with his bank account, though. He rationalized that this project was one that the entire community would see and would serve as a 3-D billboard for his business and skills.

Todd was kicking himself for screwing this up. He never should have dived into the project without verifying the budget. The allure of being Chrissy's hero had been too strong. Especially after he had jeopardized their friendship. There was nothing he wanted more than to make it up to her and recapture the closeness they had shared. A desire he had poured into every table created so far and into every hour spent planning the project.

A project that was probably nothing more than wish.

Instead of being the genie to grant Chrissy's wish, Todd mentally prepared to drop a very large hurdle in front of her dreams. Hopefully Chrissy would be able to shelve her personal feelings long enough for them to tackle it. There had to be something they could figure out to come up with the money. Not only had he failed his friend, he had failed his business. What kind of businessman started doing work without a real contract or even confirming with the client the scope of work was affordable? His dad's voice sounded sharply in his mind, reiterating Todd's own doubts. *You'll never amount to anything. Someone smarter wouldn't make this mistake. So much for school to prove yourself.*

Todd ran his hands over his face and tried to push those thoughts away. He would find Chrissy tomorrow and force her to have the conversation. It wasn't too late to save the project. Or their friendship.

TODD CONFRONTED Chrissy on Friday morning during the lull between breakfast and lunch. She tried to step around him, mumbling about an order for the kitchen, but he blocked her path.

"Chrissy, we really need to talk." Todd tried to find her eyes, but she looked past him.

"I'm sorry, Todd. I don't have time today."

His jaw clinched and he grimaced at her apathetic tone. "It's about the renovation. I promise," he held up a hand, "not to bring up anything else while we talk."

Chrissy looked at him, studied his face and then nodded. "Todd, I'm not mad at you. I know we haven't had a chance to talk, but I'm okay. Come back after lunch and I'll find some time." Todd sagged in relief at her words. There was hope.

Later, when they sat down at one of the worn booths, Chrissy looked at him expectantly. While she wasn't angry anymore, she was still working on her attitude towards him. When she looked at Todd, she was torn between memories of their sweet laughter-filled memories and the hurt she still harbored knowing he had been lying for years.

Todd took a deep breath and released it. "I should have done this weeks ago, Chris. I was so excited about this project that I never even thought about it." He rubbed his beard, a nervous habit. "I realized on Friday, when I was finishing up some work for school, that I never gave you a complete quote for the renovation. I don't know what you expected and we talked dreams and plans, but never solidified the budget, even though we picked out flooring and materials. So, with the decisions and conversations we've already had—this is the estimate." Todd slid the single sheet of paper toward her and gestured to the highlighted number in the bottom right. Watching her face, his heart broke as he saw the shock and panic in her eyes as she comprehended the number.

"T-twenty-nine th-thousand dollars?" Her voice broke in anguish.

He winced in response. "I know, I know. I'm so

sorry, Chris. I never even considered that we might be dreaming out of your price range. That's my fault. As your contractor, it was my responsibility to make sure the scope lined up with the budget." Todd felt the blame rest on his shoulders, heavier by the minute as he watched Chrissy's sweet optimistic spirit wilt in the booth across from him.

Chrissy shook the piece of paper in the air. "There's no way I can manage this, Todd. What am I going to do now? And this doesn't even include all the other things I want to do for the new place—new plates and coffee mugs and an espresso machine!" She pressed fingers to her eyes before moving them to briefly rub her temples.

"It's going to be okay, Chris. We will work it out. Here, look at this." Todd handed her the revised spreadsheet, one that had cut his margins to the bone and barely compensated him for time and labor. He explained the changes to her, and was happy to see her weak smile despite the tear-stained cheeks.

"Oh, Todd. It isn't fair to you. Especially when I've been so terrible to you. Besides, even reducing the price by eight grand doesn't make it manageable for me. We, I mean—I don't have that kind of money saved." Chrissy pushed the paper back to him.

Todd nodded. "Okay, okay. I understand. We

will make it work." He thought for a moment and then said, "You can pay me on a payment plan. Or we can do the renovations really slowly over the next year instead of all at once." He pushed the papers back toward her.

Chrissy just shook her head. "I can't owe you like that. And going slowly would ruin the whole project. Can you imagine having the nice new tables and lights, but still having the cracked linoleum? It would look cheap and half-finished for so long!" Chrissy looked at him with a sniff. "Thanks for the information, Todd. Just don't do any more work until I figure out what to do. And I'll figure out some way to pay you for what you've done so far."

CHRISSY GATHERED up the papers and made her way to the back of the cafe. Safely inside the swinging door to the kitchen, she spotted her dad sitting on a barstool at one of the stainless-steel prep tables. She burst into tears and he looked at her with fatherly concern.

"What's wrong, sweetie?"

"Oh, Dad. I don't think I can do this! I'll never have enough money to do the renovations I planned for the cafe. And I already owe Todd," she looked at the amounts listed next to the tile and lumber, "more than five thousand dollars for things he's bought and worked on!"

"Let me see that." He reached for the quotes and pulled out his reading glasses from the pocket of his shirt.

"Well, sweetie. This is a very reasonable quote." Bud gestured to the second, even lower number, "And this is down-right foolish of the boy." Softly, he added. "Todd must love you very much."

Chrissy shook her head. "That doesn't matter. Maybe he just feels sorry for me. Or it's his apology."

Bud's forehead wrinkled. "His apology for what?"

Chrissy explained the secret that Todd had been keeping from her.

"I know he hurt you, Christine. But don't be too hard on the boy. He's one of the good ones."

"Just don't, Dad. I really don't want deal with that right now. Besides, I forgave him. What I do need to do is figure out how to get him his money for the work, and figure out if there is anything I can do to make the complete renovation happen. Got any ideas?"

"Hmmm. Well, I wish your mom and I could help, but all of our money is tied up in the house in

Florida. I think your best bet is to get a loan. You should be able to go to the bank that carries the mortgage and handles our business accounts to get a renovation loan." He told her the name of the bank and gave her the name of the representative they'd always worked with. "He's a really great man, Chris. I'm sure he'll take care of it. Plus, I have all the faith in the world that you'll earn the investment back in no time with your strategy and ideas."

"Thanks, Dad. I'm going to miss you guys so much after you leave. I can't believe it is tomorrow!" The six weeks since they told her about the move had both flown by, every moment filled with plans and lists.

"We are always just a phone call away, okay? You can call us any time."

Chrissy gave her Dad a hug and sent him home to help her mom finish packing. Then, she sat in the kitchen for a very long time, looking at the spreadsheets.

15

Todd watched Chrissy walk away from the booth they'd shared. Her normal bounce was notably absent and he hated that he had been the one to do that to her. He was sure it wasn't just the shock of the quoted total. It was also the lies, and the transformation of their friendship into a cold remnant of what it had been just a few weeks before.

Todd was tempted to just pay for the renovations. After all, he had money saved up. He'd gotten a surprising amount when his father had passed away. Probably some life insurance policy his father had forgotten about, otherwise it surely would have been cashed out early.

Still, the money remained untouched.

Todd despised his father and didn't want

anything from him ever again. The money sitting in his account would be more than enough to pay for Chrissy's renovation and all the extras she wanted. He'd buy her the best espresso machine on the market if it meant she would look at him again like she had under the mistletoe. But he knew she would never accept the money and he felt pathetic even thinking about trying to buy her affection. Like the woman in Proverbs 31, Chrissy was worth more than rubies or gold.

Instead, he prayed God would show him how to make things right between them, and that God would give Chrissy guidance on how to tackle this obstacle. The renovation had to happen somehow. He thought the cafe might not survive without it and he definitely didn't think Chrissy would stick around if the cafe was the same as it had always been. She needed to put her stamp on it. And Todd couldn't think of anything he wanted more than to spend the next two months making her dreams for the bistro come true. *Plus, it wouldn't hurt to have that time to convince her I'm not such a bad guy, despite my mistakes. If I was here every day, working alongside her, maybe we could move forward again.*

Todd finally got up from the booth and returned to his workshop. Despite Chrissy's instructions to quit working on her project until he got the go ahead, he was going to finish the tables. If nothing else, he thought the new tables and a paint job would give the cafe a much-needed face lift, regardless of what Chrissy said about the renovations being 'all or nothing.'

CHRISSY SPENT the rest of Friday night and the entire weekend fretting over how she would find the money for the renovation. She debated every possible option and finally agreed she would have to take out a loan. She ran some rough numbers on the additional funds she would require to make the bistro a reality. After the morning rush on Monday, Chrissy sat down at an empty booth armed with the cafe's most recent monthly statements and the total required loan number. She dialed the number she had for the bank, located in Chicago.

An automated menu greeted her and she obediently responded to the prompts. Finally, a cheery female voice greeted her. "Hello, you've reached Business Services. How may I help you today?"

"Umm, hello. This is Christine Mathes from Bud and Janine's Cafe in Minden, Indiana. I am calling to speak with Dennis Cochran about a new business loan." Christine forced confidence into her voice. *I am a competent business owner.*

"Okay. All new business loans need to be handled in person, Ms. Mathes. Let me check the calendar, just one moment." Chrissy's heart sank. *In person? I have to go to Chicago? No way. No way.* The voice returned, "Miss Mathes? Looks like next week is going to be very tricky with the Christmas holiday coming up. I'm afraid the first availability our loan officer has will be the following week—on December 27th. Will that work for you?"

Chrissy hesitated, dreading the thought of going to Chicago. She hadn't been back since she had stopped attending class and failed out. She squeezed her eyes shut and pictured the bistro, finished and full of customers enjoying the new food and atmosphere. With her eyes still closed, as though it would give her courage, she finally spoke. "I'll be there."

"Great. Our loan officer will need to see the business plan, six months of recent statements, and any other relevant documentation related to the loan you will be seeking."

Chrissy was glad the conversation ended without much input needed from her. She was still processing two things. One: she was going to Chicago. And two: she needed an official business plan. She tried not to panic at the thought of either. She thought, perhaps naively, all it would take was a simple phone call to the bank and a short discussion with this Mr. Cochran and he would happily write her a check for thirty thousand dollars. At the realization of what she was asking for, she snorted. *Of course they wouldn't just hand over thirty grand! I am ridiculous to have even thought it would be the case. But now, I have to go to Chicago. And there is no one to go with me.* The thought of being alone in the city filled Chrissy with panic and dread. *I'll be all alone, just like I was that night.* Before she could stop them, the memories bombarded her.

CHRISSY WALKED toward her dorm from one of the late-night coffee shops. Insisting she was fine, she had declined her friends' offers for a ride. It was a nice night, slightly chilly, but clear and not too windy. It was nearly 11 pm and although it was a Thursday night, the bars that catered to the college crowd were busy. Passing the door to one such bar, Chrissy could hear the music grow louder as a group of guys stumbled out of the door. She kept walking when they called out.

A loud voice called out, "Hey baby."

Keep walking. Chrissy's heart surged.

"You going home all alone tonight?" The man's voice was loose, words slurring together as he yelled at her retreating figure.

Chrissy readjusted the strap of her bookbag and tried to walk a bit faster without being too noticeable.

A different voice this time, "Come on, baby, don't be like that. We just want to talk."

Chrissy was freaked out at this point and began to pray earnestly. *Please, God, just let me get home safely.* But God remained silent and the men did not. Suddenly, Chrissy felt her bag being ripped from her shoulder. It hit the ground and she took a step in an attempt to run, but felt a strong grip on her upper arm, whipping her around. Three men surrounded her as she looked desperately in all directions for an avenue of escape.

"Not so fast, sweetheart. Why you gotta ignore us, huh? A pudgy girl like you ought to appreciate the attention."

The tallest of the men leered at her, "You're pretty cute for a chubby girl, you know."

One of them—she remembered his goatee and

greasy hair—spoke up next. "I don't mind a little meat on 'em, boys. Makes 'em eager to please. I'll bet this one gives it good." Chrissy pulled away as he reached out, put his hands on her waist, and tried to pull her close. The other two men laughed at her response.

"I don't think she likes you, JP."

"Yeah, seems like she isn't *eager to please* you!" The tall man taunted his friend.

The one they called JP growled at the ridicule of his friends. "Come on, I'm gonna teach this little witch a lesson." The other two men cheered in agreement and herded her toward the alley.

Chrissy struggled against their strong grip and began to yell. "Help! Help me. Somebody, help!"

One of the men, the biggest one, quickly pulled her hair and covered her mouth with his hand. "Shut your mouth, or I'll shut it for you." With her face pointed to the sky, and tears of pain and fear filling her eyes, she was pulled into the alley.

They continued their taunts of her weight and their threats if she were to scream or report what had happened. When she finally quit fighting and resigned herself to her fate, they praised what a good girl she was. Chrissy squeezed her eyes shut, desperate to escape.

They finished their fun, then they left Chrissy

with her clothes ripped and her body covered in bruises. She curled up against the cold brick wall of the alley and stared at a single brick, silently crying for what seemed like hours. All alone in the chill of the winter night. All alone in the darkness of the alley. All alone.

CHRISSY SHUDDERED out of the memory and thought once more of the upcoming trip to Chicago. She would be alone in the big city once again if she went to the bank to get this loan. Her breathing became rapid and shallow as she fought back tears. Struggling to take a deeper breath, she laid her head down on the table and prayed.

16

Todd felt remarkably light and cheery as he walked down Main Street toward Bud and Janine's. Finals were over, the entire quote situation was out in the open with Chrissy. Yesterday was the first time he was able to attend church without the weight of his secret casting a cloud on his mood, an he'd slept better last night than he had in ages.

Main Street was fully decked out for Christmas, just one week away. The planters held miniature pine trees decorated with multi-colored ornaments and lights. Banners with snowflakes, snowmen, 'Merry Christmas', and 'Happy New Year' hung from the street lights. The shop windows were decorated with vintage toy train villages, blankets of fluffy fake snow, and Christmas trees of all shapes and sizes. The bakery, owned by a sweet older lady named Margaret, displayed delicious looking cookies and pies, and Todd made a mental note to stop by after lunch to buy a snowflake sugar cookie. He took a satisfied breath of the brisk winter air. Yep, it was a wonderful day. Now, he just needed the renovation expenses to be worked out and everything would be right as rain.

Todd entered the cafe and was surprised to see Chrissy sitting at one of the booths. She had papers in front of her and her cell phone in hand. But her head was resting on her forearm and she wasn't moving. Walking over to the booth, he knocked on the table.

"Hey Chris. You okay?"

"Go away." She spoke directly into the laminate table top and the sound was muffled.

"Ah, come on. Whatever it is can't be that bad."

Chrissy lifted her head. Splotchy cheeks and puffy, watery eyes rimmed with red stared back at him. She sniffed. "I'm not going to get a loan for the renovations."

Todd sat down across from her, "The bank already said no? I'm so sorry, Chris. They are missing a huge opportunity." He fought the urge to reach for her hand.

Chrissy was silent for a second. "They didn't really say no..." Trailing off, she laid her head back down.

"What do you mean?"

"The bank is in Chicago. I can't go to Chicago!" Again, Chrissy was talking directly to the table instead of to Todd.

Todd considered that for a moment. He had no idea why Chrissy thought she couldn't go to Chicago. She had gone to school there for a year and a half before coming back home. Todd figured she had run out of money for tuition. The way she was talking, the mafia had chased her out of the city.

Chrissy lifted her head, "Unless..." A glimmer of hope shined behind smeared mascara.

Todd lifted an eyebrow.

She continued, "Unless you come with me?"

"What?" The shock was evident in his voice. It was the last thing he expected her to say. They'd been fighting for weeks. Chrissy was avoiding him like a sticky spot on the cafe floor, and now she wanted him to go to Chicago with her?

She wiped her eyes and looked up at him from under wet lashes. "Come with me to Chicago, Todd.

Please?" He studied her red face as she pleaded with him and Todd knew that he would do anything for this woman. She was his best friend. And God help him, he loved her.

Todd cataloged his ongoing projects and considered the upcoming holiday. Actual plans for Christmas were nonexistent, and most of his contractor jobs would be on hold for the holidays anyway. What would a couple of days in Chicago with Chrissy be like? Trying not to smile too brightly, he removed his coat and sat it in the booth next to him. "When do we leave?"

CHRISSY WAS BOTH INCREDIBLY RELIEVED that Todd was going to go with her to Chicago and mortified that she had asked him at all. She didn't see another option at this point, though. She needed this loan, which meant she was going to Chicago. With Todd. It was hard to stay mad at him when he was always so willing to help. He hadn't even questioned why she couldn't go to the city without him. Just flashed one of his trademark grins and agreed to come.

After the attack, Chrissy had tried to move

forward. But, instead of going to classes, she found herself buried under her blankets and barely able to leave her dorm room. She went without eating or showering, stopped returning calls from her friends, and couldn't go to church. God, if he was even real, had abandoned her in that alley and the thought of hearing worship songs made her want to throw up. When she'd finally been forced to leave school after failing all her classes, she'd gone home. For years after returning, she'd put on a brave face. She was friendly at the cafe, but she still avoid church— always volunteering to do the prep work before the cafe opened.

When Rachel died, it seemed like more proof that God didn't care. As she watched Miss Ruth grieve her daughter, though, she wasn't so sure. Ruth was hurting but, somehow, still at peace. Ruth wasn't angry at God. In fact, she seemed closer to God than ever. Rachel's husband, Luke, on the other hand, was angry and withdrawn and bitter. She'd never seen him like that before. So, for the first time in over three years, she had prayed. God used those short, limited prayers for Luke to reach Chrissy too. As Chrissy prayed for Luke's anger and bitterness to be healed, God healed her own bitterness. He revealed his grace to her and while she knew she would never understand fully why God hadn't stopped her attack or Rachel's accident, Chrissy was no longer angry and depressed.

Chrissy embraced her life in Minden and her work at the cafe. That was two years ago. She still hadn't gone further than Terre Haute alone since then out of fear, but always reassured herself she didn't mind. *Life is good here in Minden. I don't mind if I never go anywhere else again. I trust people here. The Travel Channel and my books are just as good as seeing the world in person. And much better than going back to Chicago—ever again.* The money she'd saved to travel was going to go to paying Todd for the work he'd already done.

Now she was looking at a total of six or more hours in the car with him on the way to and from the city, not to mention the time they would actually spend there. Pushing aside the thought, Chrissy gathered her papers from the table, and grabbed a few napkins from the dispenser to wipe her nose and eyes. She had to get back to Norm in the kitchen. It was his first day and she'd left him for far too long to call the bank.

Norm had worked with her this morning during

breakfast and had done a great job. Breakfast was pretty easy, though. They made a couple of large trays of biscuits and a large batch of pancake batter together. Once she showed him where to find the eggs, bacon and sausage he was able to prep most of the orders without much input from her, which left her free to take orders and handle coffee refills without feeling too overwhelmed. She had worked breakfast in the past trying to handle both customers and cooking, and it always made her feel like customers were waiting too long and she was constantly behind. But Norm was a pro and the pancakes came out fluffy and the eggs cooked perfectly to order.

It was nearly time for the lunch crowd, and she hadn't even covered the menu with Norm. She paused at the restroom to splash some cool water on her face in an attempt to disguise the fact that she'd been crying and pushed into the kitchen.

Norm had cleaned up from breakfast and was busy stirring something that smelled delicious in a big pot. He smiled at her warmly as she walked in. "I was wondering where you'd run off to."

"Sorry about that. I had a phone call to make. What are you making?" She lifted onto her toes to peer into the tall pot he stirred.

"Well, on a chilly day like today, I figured a hearty soup would hit the spot, so I whipped up some creamy chicken and noodle while I had time. Here, have a taste." He grabbed a tasting spoon from the container on the counter and held a spoonful out to her, with a hand cupped under it. She blew on the steaming spoon and the scent of thyme and garlic hit her nose. After a taste, she had to admit it was some of the best soup she'd ever tasted.

"Wow, that's fantastic. Did we have everything you needed?"

Norm tossed the spoon into the sink. "Oh yeah, I just kind of dug through the kitchen until I found enough to pull something together. Soup is easy."

"Well, it's great. I can't wait to tell everyone that we have it on special for lunch. Speaking of lunch, time got away from me. I'll just run you through the basics and we will deal with anything odd as it comes up."

Chrissy showed him everything for burgers and sandwiches, and laughed at his dismay when she showed him the pre-made chicken and tuna salads.

"I know it isn't ideal, but that's what mom and dad always served. If we have tuna or chicken salad on the bistro menu, I'd like it to be homemade so it can have a little more unique flair. For now, we buy premade, and we doctor up each serving before making the sandwich. A little fresh diced pickle, some salt and pepper and a squeeze of lemon makes it a thousand times better than straight from the can."

Norm was nodding his understanding. "Okay then. I don't love it, but I'll make it work for now."

Chrissy smiled. They continued their short walk-through of the kitchen and Chrissy heard the bells jingle over the door, indicating more customers. She hated those stupid bells, but had to admit they were handy when she was in the back of the restaurant. "I'll go take orders and let you do your thing. If you see an order you don't understand, let me know." Chrissy reached the door and looked back. "Norm, I'm really glad you're here. Seriously."

He smiled and started pulling things out of the refrigerator to set up a sandwich station on one counter. Chrissy said another silent prayer of thanks for God sending Norm to her. He could probably be a chef anywhere, and she was going to do everything in her power to make sure he would stay there with her. She grabbed her apron off the hook by the door to the kitchen and felt her ponytail to make sure the pen she had stashed there earlier was still in place. She eyed the tables and began filling water glasses to take over with her.

"Hey Jimmy. Hey Earl. You staying warm today? We've got some awesome homemade creamy chicken noodle soup back there that'll chase the chill away for a bit. Can I start you with a cup?"

17

*B*y Friday, Chrissy felt like she and Norm had been working together for years. He had a fatherly manner about him, despite his admission to never having kids of his own. Norm's ability to jump right in was a lifesaver, since Chrissy and Todd would leave for Chicago on Saturday. While they were gone Mandy had agreed to fill in as waitress. It seemed that buzz about the cafe's new chef was getting around and business was good all week, especially considering the time of year and cold weather.

Even Miss Ruth ventured out to meet Luke for lunch. Chrissy greeted them both warmly, and recommended the day's special. Norm had made homemade chicken pot pie, which they both decided to order without a glance at the rest of the menu. Chrissy put in the order and went to refill drinks for a table of retired farmers who often lingered for hours. They always cracked jokes and made Chrissy laugh. When Norm came out of the kitchen to deliver the plates to Ruth and Luke, Chrissy quickly excused herself from the table of regulars and came over to help Norm.

Norm waved off her help. "Just wanted to make sure they got it while it was still hot, and I know those fellas can talk your ear off."

"No, no, it's great. Thanks for doing that. Norm, these are my friends." She gestured to the lively redhead and her son-in-law, "Miss Ruth and Luke. This is Norman, my new chef. You are in for a huge treat." Chrissy feigned a whisper, placing her hand on one side of her mouth and leaning in toward the table, "He's even better than my dad."

"Nice to meet you, Norman," said Miss Ruth in her gentle way.

"The pleasure is all mine. Please call me Norm." He shook her hand, watching her face.

After a few seconds, Luke cleared his throat when Norm had yet to turn to him. "Yep, nice to meet you, Norm. Thanks for the food." Still, Norm glanced at Luke for a few brief seconds before looking back at Ruth. Luke and Chrissy made eye contact and shared an amused smile.

Norm made his way back to the kitchen and Chrissy stayed at the table to chat.

"What's Charlotte up to today?" Luke and Charlotte seemed inseparable. They were definitely in the engagement-bliss phase of their relationship. The wedding was scheduled for just over a month away. After the interviews ended, Chrissy hadn't really seen Charlotte much.

"She's got a conference call with Ascension today to discuss what their expectations are and how they anticipate using her services next year. Basically, she is still working out the details of what it means for her to transition from corporate recruiting to ministry staffing." Luke spoke with pride about his future wife. Charlotte had spent weeks clearing her name from the scandal that brought her to Minden with a career in shambles. Then, she had discovered that she could use her gifts and corporate experience in a completely different way. Charlotte would be working for an agency that helped large churches find pastors and executive leadership.

Chrissy was thrilled for her friend. Charlotte had been devastated when her career had collapsed, her retreat to Minden being less voluntary than prescribed. "Oh, that's great. I just think it is so amazing how God brought that opportunity for her."

Ruth chimed in, "Absolutely."

Luke changed the subject then. "I heard you are going to Chicago with Todd? I guess you aren't upset with him anymore?"

Chrissy shifted her weight and fidgeted with the pen in her hand. "Yeah, he is coming to Chicago with me so I can go to the bank. I really didn't want to go alone." She shrugged. "And, yes. I guess I'm not really mad at him. He must have told you all what happened?" At their nods of confirmation, she continued, "I just thought that I would be someone he told, you know? We've been friends for so long." Her shoulders dropped. "It just sucked that he kept such a big secret." Chrissy thought back to the kisses they shared and the road they'd been walking down before his dishonesty came to light. She might not be mad at him anymore, but things were definitely not back to where they were.

Maybe they couldn't be again.

Chrissy smiled at their understanding faces. "Well, let me get out of your hair so you can enjoy your lunch. Let me know if you need anything at all."

Luke swallowed the bite he'd been eating. "Thanks, Chrissy. It's really good, by the way."

Ruth nodded and blushed, "Be sure to tell Norm how much we are enjoying it."

Chrissy couldn't help but smile as she walked back to the kitchen. Ruth and Norm? Now that could be interesting. Ruth's husband had died nearly twenty years earlier and Chrissy couldn't remember Ruth dating, or even being interested in anyone. She was a beautiful woman in her mid-fifties, but she could easily pass for forty-five.

Chrissy wondered if Luke would be okay with it. He hadn't seemed too disturbed by the exchange at the table, though. Ruth wasn't technically his mother, but from everything Chrissy knew, Ruth was the closest thing Luke had to one. He tended to be protective of her. Either way, if it came down to it, Chrissy already knew that she would vouch for Norm as a decent guy. He was whistling in the kitchen as she grabbed an order from the window and she couldn't help but smile. Everything was going to be okay. *I'll go to Chicago and get the loan, and Norm and I will serve delicious food to everyone in Minden. And Todd will renovate the space to a beautiful bistro.*

Despite Todd's willingness to come with her to Chicago, she still wasn't over the hurt. Chrissy was trying not to remember all the fun they'd had over the last few weeks before the fight. She reminded herself that it wasn't him; Todd was a different guy than she knew. One with a college degree—or most of one anyway—and one who could work circles around her on a computer and design amazing furniture. He wasn't the friend she'd known since elementary school she'd kissed after he told corny jokes.

Her eyes landed on the mistletoe hanging above the kitchen door.

And there will be absolutely no more kissing.

*W*ith Christmas the following Monday, Chrissy planned to be at the bank early on Tuesday morning. There was a big snow storm predicted to hit Indiana on Christmas Eve and Christmas Day. Since she didn't have any plans, and neither did Todd, they decided to drive to Chicago on Saturday morning to be safe. The cafe would be closed for the holiday, and it would give them time to scope out the city. They even talked about finding a church to attend a Christmas Eve service if the weather held out. She'd love to go to a candlelit service if they could find it—just like in Minden.

Todd spent the week wrapping up small projects. He laid tile in the Richard's bathroom, and painted the living room at Mr. and Mrs. Parks' house. These were all projects that needed to be finished before the holiday, each hosting Christmas celebrations at their house. Todd tried not to be jealous at the thought of the happy families gathered around the Christmas trees he saw decorated in their homes. He pushed the thought of a cozy fire and eggnog away when he saw stockings hanging from the mantle. He would be with Chrissy.

While a bleak hotel in Chicago might not be the homey image he imagined for Christmas, Todd was determined to make it special. This was Chrissy's first Christmas without her parents and she was bound to be lonely.

Todd, on the other hand, was used to it. Some years, he would go to Miss Ruth's and enjoy the idyllic Christmas he never had as a kid—too many Christmas cookies, beautifully wrapped gifts under the tree, and Christmas carols playing softly in the background during a hearty dinner. It wasn't his family, though and it tempered his enjoyment just enough. Todd couldn't wait for the day when his own kids and wife were laughing over hot cocoa or listening with rapt attention as he read the story of Jesus' birth from the family Bible.

Christmas in Chicago? Todd figured there was

probably some huge Christmas tree to go see. Or maybe they could volunteer somewhere. As far as he knew, they didn't even have a hotel room booked. Maybe that would be a good place to start. Todd checked with Chrissy and she confirmed that she hadn't even thought about making a reservation. So, Todd started planning. He was going to make this Christmas special for both of them. And try his best to recapture some of the magic between them. Christmas was a time for miracles, right?

EVEN THOUGH TODD would be coming with her, Chrissy grew more and more apprehensive and fearful as the trip grew closer. Saturday morning arrived and she was a nervous wreck but trying hard to hide the reason from Todd.

"I'm just nervous about talking to the bank," she lied, tearing at a jagged nail with her teeth.

Todd seemed unusually excited about the trip as he herded her into his truck. "It's going to be wonderful, Chris. You'll do great. And we have more than two whole days before we have to worry about that. Let's just go enjoy the city."

Christmas carols played as they made the drive into Chicago. There was quite a bit of traffic but thankfully, the weather was clear. They chatted a bit on the drive, but often sat in companionable silence. Chrissy was grateful that Todd was driving, because even though she had lived in the city for over a year, she didn't like driving there and never felt confident navigating. Todd seemed to know where he was going as he took an exit from the expressway. They drove down Lake Shore Drive, looking out over the frigid waters of Lake Michigan. The both shook their heads at the dedicated joggers who insisted on running, even in stocking hats and gloves.

When Chrissy asked where they were staying, Todd's only reply was, "You'll see."

Before long, Todd turned off Lake Shore Drive and a few blocks later, pulled into the valet lane of what seemed to Chrissy to be a very fancy hotel. A man opened the door for Chrissy and helped her down from the truck as Todd began unloading their suitcases from the back. Todd gestured with an arm for her to proceed ahead of him through the large revolving door. When she exited on the other side, Chrissy stopped short, barely out of the path of the swinging door. Todd carefully maneuvered the bags around her and pulled her off to one side so they wouldn't block the door.

He watched her eyes and face carefully as she took in all the details of the ornate hotel lobby. The Palmer House Hotel was Chicago's oldest—built in the 1870s. The building screamed extravagance, even 130 years later. The floors were marble, with huge oriental rugs breaking up the space filled with small seating arrangements and potted plants. Soaring columns ran nearly three stories to the lobby ceiling, which was decorated with intricate paintings of Greek Mythology. Grand marble staircases led to different levels within the open space. Rich, dark mahogany woodwork was decorated with garland and Christmas lights, and several massive Christmas trees were scattered throughout the expansive space and the surrounding balcony level. Every coffee and end table had sprigs of winter greenery and red candles or gold bows, and potted poinsettias nearly three feet in diameter graced the landing of the main staircase.

"Wow," she breathed. Chrissy felt like there was nothing more to say.It was the most beautiful building Chrissy had ever seen and the added Christmas ambiance made it magical.

Todd watched her take in the space, her eyes

dancing from corner to corner, up to the ceiling and over every inch. He tried to memorize the way the warm twinkle of lights reflected in her blue eyes, and soaked in the wide smile on her face. He had done all kinds of research trying to decide where to stay for this trip, and though he'd never stayed in a place that cost this much money before, it was worth it just for the look on Chrissy's face.

She finally looked up at him. "We're staying here? It's amazing. But... Todd. We can't afford this."

Todd kicked a foot and looked down at the ground. "I wanted to do this for you. It's my treat." He looked back at her, vulnerable.

Chrissy desperately wanted to accept his gift. It would be a dream come true to stay in a historic place like this. But she was already here in Chicago because she didn't have money to pay him for the work she wanted him to do. It hardly seemed wise to accept such an extravagant hotel room when a room in the suburbs for eighty bucks a night would work just as well.

Just then, she watched a group of people proceed down the stairs from the balcony and assemble in rows on one of the staircases. A single note rang out and they began to sing. And Chrissy knew that she couldn't leave. She smiled at Todd and nodded. With a whisper, she added, "Okay," and notes of "White Christmas" followed them as they made their way to the check-in desk. When Todd gave them his name, the clerk pulled up the reservation and immediately straightened his posture. "Of course, Mr. Flynn. Welcome to the Palmer House. We're so glad you could join us. We have you in the Abbott Suite for your stay."

Chrissy's eyes widened at the announcement they would be in a suite. The young man fumbled through a stack of paperwork and pulled out a small folder. He spoke with a polite, business-like tone. "Here are your room keys, sir. Breakfast is available in the restaurant each morning. Of course, room service is also available. You can find that information in your suite. There is complementary bottled water in your suite, as well as a bottle of Champagne courtesy of our Manager. Can I get you or Mrs. Flynn anything else right now?" Chrissy looked between the clerk and her friend. This was too much. Why were they getting such special treatment? The clerk thought they were married. Should she correct him?

Instead of correcting his assumption, Todd simply shook his head. "No, thank you. This is great."

The young man pressed his hands together.

"Wonderful. Let me call our porter, Damien, over. He will take your bags and escort you to your room and show you all the features and amenities in the suite. Please enjoy your stay, Mr. Flynn. My name is Tristan. If you need anything at all, please don't hesitate to call."

19

They walked through the grand lobby on their way to the elevators, with Damien leading the way. Chrissy continued to soak in the sound of the small choir singing Christmas songs and the exquisitely decorated historic hotel. Damien told them a little of the history of the hotel during the ride in the elevator. Chrissy was entranced with his colorful story-telling. Damien opened the door to their room and gestured for her to enter before him. The room was far bigger than her apartment at home. Walking in, her eyes widened at the sight of a large dining room table, seating area with a couch and multiple arm chairs. The furnishings were updated, but still complemented the feel of the historic hotel. Damien set their bags near the table and showed them the kitchen area, with a stocked fridge and champagne glasses displayed next to a bottle of champagne already chilling on ice.

Then, the porter grabbed their bags again and walked them from the main area into one of several doors Chrissy could see. This led to a large bedroom with a king-size bed, where he placed the suitcases on a bench near the dresser. He pointed out the thermostat and the connected bathroom before leading them back into the living area. He gestured to the remote control sitting next to the large-screen television. There was an awkward few seconds while Damien tried to think of anything else they might need and seemed to linger for a bit.

Todd suddenly moved toward the door while discretely pulling a bill from his wallet. He palmed the cash and shook Damien's hand, like he had seen the rich and famous do in movies. Damien nodded and took his exit, leaving them alone in the large space.

Todd sighed, relieved to be free of the porter. He wasn't used to the VIP treatment he seemed to be getting. He'd only booked the suite because it was the only option for two separate bedrooms. At the thought Todd quickly went to the bedroom and removed his suitcase from where it sat next to Chrissy's. He carried it to the other bedroom, which was tucked behind the kitchenette and featured two Queen beds. The bathroom was not connected to the bedroom, but was accessible from the main area. He wanted to give Chrissy the King Size bed, and the privacy of the en suite bathroom. When he walked back into the living room, Chrissy was leaning against the counter top.

"What's with the fancy digs, Flynn?" She raised an eyebrow at him.

Todd shuffled his feet and admitted, "We needed two bedrooms, but I didn't want us to be separated. In case you needed me or something."

Immediately, Chrissy relaxed. "Thanks for thinking of that. I wouldn't have wanted to be too far away either. This room is amazing, isn't it? Do I even want to know how much it cost?"

Todd shook his head. "Not a chance. But it is worth it. You are worth it, Chris." Todd was standing in front of her now, and looked at her very intently, trying to convey something with a look that he couldn't verbalize yet. *I'd give you everything, Christine Mathes. If only I thought you would accept it.*

～

CHRISSY, uncomfortable with the intensity of his gaze, slid to the right and escaped from her place between Todd and the counter top. She wandered the room and looked out the windows, pleased to see the city sprawling out in front of her. The last twenty minutes had overwhelmed her a bit. This room was incredible and so was the hotel. And Todd? He had done this for her. Todd didn't even know about her fear of the city but had guessed that she wouldn't want to be alone in a hotel room. And sharing a room wasn't an option—even with separate beds. Although it made her wonder what it would be like to wake up in the middle of the night and hear him breathing less than ten feet away. *I wonder if he snores?* The question made her smile. If they shared a room, she would probably hear Todd showering in the next room in the morning. The thought of something so intimate made her blush.

Chrissy tried to push away the thought of Todd with no clothes. As it was, he would only be across the suite. Again, she marveled at his generosity and kindness. She had no idea how much this room cost, but it had to be a few thousand dollars for the length of their stay. She would never be able to repay Todd for everything he was doing. He was missing Christmas, for crying out loud! Chrissy turned from the window to study him instead of the city. Todd fiddled with the remote and managed to turn on something sports related. Then, he walked to the kitchenette and reached into the refrigerator. Todd closed the fridge, holding two water bottles, before he looked at her and noticed her watching him.

"Water?"

"Thanks," she said, taking one of the bottles.

Todd settled into a corner of the couch and took off his shoes before propping his feet up on the coffee table. Chrissy envied his ability to be completely at ease wherever he was. Todd just belonged. Whether it was helping move haybales, on a construction site, sitting in a church pew, or—apparently—tipping a bellboy and residing in a penthouse suite in one of the fanciest hotels in Chicago. Self-assured and confident. Any observer would think Todd stayed in places like this every day.

Chrissy never felt that comfortable in her own skin. Even before the night in the alley, she felt frumpy and awkward. She was happy and cheerful most of the time, but there was always an edge of self-doubt. In school, despite her academic achievements, she worried her peers didn't like her. Even the decision of where to sit at church, she worried she would offend someone or steal their seat. Chrissy tried to remember ever making a decision with complete confidence and her mind went to the discussion with Todd about the renovations for the bistro.

With his encouragement, she felt completely solid in the design decisions she made for her space. Without his confidence in her, would she feel the same surety in her own choices? Even with the inner conviction of turning the cafe into something that was entirely her own, self-doubt chased her. Todd's confidence made her shake her head. But it also filled her with happiness. Chrissy didn't understand what he saw in her, but she was sure grateful it meant she had him as a friend. But a friend was all he could be. He had to see how different they were, and how much better he was. Todd had kept his promise and hadn't mentioned anything about the fight or the kisses. Clearly, he finally agreed that they weren't meant to be. Chrissy should be relieved. Instead, she found herself watching her friend, laughing at the hole in the bottom of his sock and jealous of the woman who would eventually hear him showering in the next room.

It was tempting to take a nap, but Todd forced himself off the couch and talked Chrissy into venturing out. They were close to Willis Tower, the tallest building in Chicago, so they decided to walk there. On the way, they grabbed hot chocolate at a small coffee shop and admired the displays in the windows of little shops and restaurants. Chrissy took some pictures so she could recreate some aspects of the displays next Christmas at the bistro. They bought tickets for the SkyDeck and stood in line for the elevators. Once they were on the 103rd floor, Todd tried desperately to hide his fear of heights. He stood well away from the glass boxes that extended from the wall of the building. Chrissy, on the other hand, was gleefully taking in the experience. When she realized that Todd was no longer next to her as she stood and looked at the city laid out under her feet, she tore her gaze from the microscopic cars and searched for him.

She found him tucked against the wall in a small alcove. "Come on! What are you doing?"

"I'm good over here," he assured her. "Look, there is our hotel." Todd tried to distract her, but it didn't last long.

"Oh, come on. You're not scared of heights, are you?"

"Of course I'm not scared of heights." Todd gave her a crooked grin. "I'm scared of falling, which is a perfectly rational fear."

Chrissy laughed. "You're not going to fall." She grabbed his upper arm. "Come on, you can hold on to me."

That sounded like a pretty good offer, so Todd reluctantly followed her into the glass box. *Don't look down. Don't look down.* He looked down and immediately tried to pull back toward the carpeted floor of the SkyDeck, but Chrissy's grip on his arm tightened.

"Look at how little the cars are, Todd." He heard the same cheerful tone in her voice he'd been missing for weeks.

He closed his eyes and took a deep breath. Then he opened them and tried to focus on the cars. Quickly, Todd became fascinated by trying to identify different objects. Trees, cars, and even rooftop swimming pools all appeared the size of dollhouse fixtures. Chrissy stepped away from him to look in another direction and his unease returned. He stepped out of the glass enclosure and watched Chrissy enjoy the view. Her smile never failed to lift his spirits. If it was something that he had done to make her smile, he felt ten feet tall, as though everything was right in the world. It scared him a little bit how much power her happiness had over his own. For now, though, he would do everything he could to make her smile. Todd would just enjoy that she was no longer holding his dishonesty against him.

After Willis Tower, they walked to Millennium Park. It was getting close to dinner, and Todd suggested an early bite to eat. The fast food they'd grabbed before reaching the city was hours ago and he was starving. After a quick search, they settled on a little Mexican restaurant. The restaurant was a little more upscale than the typical places in Terre Haute or Greencastle. The waiter made them fresh guacamole from a cart rolled next to their table, and there were three types of salsa to try with their chips. Todd felt like it was victory when they decided to split an order of fajitas. Sharing an entree seemed reserved for close friends and couples. Maybe it meant they were getting back to where they had been.

The food was fantastic and Todd couldn't help but feel like this was more of a date than they had ever been on. He didn't vocalize that thought to Chrissy, but he knew he wanted to repeat the experience. Chrissy passed him the sour cream before he could even ask for it, and he caught the server's eye when he noticed her soda getting low. It was as though they'd shared a hundred intimate dinners together.

Like any good tourists, they took pictures in front of the famous "Bean" sculpture after dinner. Luckily, it wasn't quite dark yet. The park's outdoor skating rink was busy, but not packed. Todd quickly agreed to skating after he saw Chrissy's eyes light up at the sight of the rink. They changed into the rental skates and Chrissy eagerly skated off, leaving him behind on the bench. He watched her for a moment. The ends of her pink scarf trailed behind her and she gracefully dodged a small child who fell a few feet in front of her. He watched her approach as she completed her first lap. The chill in the air and the exertion from skating left her delicate cheeks and nose tinged with pink. Chrissy smiled broadly and skated back to him, pulling 5him to his feet.

As they started to skate, she didn't remove her gloved hand from his. He was much slower than her and not nearly as graceful. Silently, he thanked God that he hadn't yet fallen, then continued with a plea that he would stay on his skates as they rounded the first corner. Todd had competed in traditional sports —basketball, baseball, and football—but, hockey wasn't exactly big in their corner of rural Indiana, so he had only been on ice skates a time or two. He quickly caught on and his confidence grew. Still, Todd held her hand and relished the feeling. Chrissy seemed like a natural on the ice. They continued lap after lap and enjoyed watching the small children, sometimes pointing out someone doing turns and jumps in the center of the rink. There were lots of couples, skating hand-in-hand and the picture of sweet romance. Todd figured he and Chrissy must look much the same at the moment.

From the skating rink they could see the enormous Christmas tree lit up for the holiday. It had to be nearly sixty feet tall and was covered in thousands of lights. They decided to return their skates and head back to the hotel. As darkness fell, lights from the tree and others scattered among the bare trees in the park illuminated the area. Walking past the Christmas tree, Todd remembered what he had read when researching for the trip.

"Did you know that each year, people nominate trees to be chosen as the official Chicago Christmas tree? People have to submit pictures and say why they think it should win. It's got to be a minimum of fifty feet tall and only certain types of trees are eligible. Plus, it has to be within one hundred miles of Chicago. Once it is chosen, they go chop it down to bring it here."

Chrissy stared up at the tree. "That's crazy! How many fifty-foot-tall trees can there be?"

"One less every year, I guess", Todd joked, and Chrissy rolled her eyes at him.

"I can't even think of one near Minden anywhere close to that big. I bet it is pretty hard to find. And then they take an old, beautiful tree that has stood for probably hundreds of years and chop it down?"

Todd considered that. "That's true. But think of how many people get to enjoy the tree after they bring it into the city. Way more than would ever get to appreciate it if it was left in the forest to get knocked down by a tornado or struck by lightning or something."

"Hmmm. That's true. It is really pretty. There is something special about a tree all decked out to celebrate the holiday."

"I agree. I never appreciated Christmas until I became a Christian," Todd said. "It was never all that special growing up. But now, I don't think any party could be big enough when I realize it is all to celebrate Jesus coming to earth as a baby."

Their celebration was certainly unorthodox this year. Instead of spending it with family, or even their church at home, they were here in this strange city. "Let's make sure we go to church tomorrow night. I'm sure we can find a Christmas Eve service some-

where. I'm sorry we aren't back in Minden to celebrate with everyone else."

Todd smiled. "That sounds perfect, Chris. I don't
really mind being here instead. At least I'm with
you," he said with a blush.

----

20

*W*hen they got back to the hotel room, Chrissy quickly retreated to her bedroom with the excuse of wanting a shower and to fall into bed early. She took an excessively long shower and used three towels to dry off, determined to enjoy every bit of luxury this hotel could provide. Lying in the luxurious linens before succumbing to sleep, Chrissy pulled out her Bible and read a few chapters. When Chrissy finally awoke on Christmas Eve, she was appalled at her hair, which was sticking out in all directions due to falling asleep with it wet. She quickly tamed it into a low ponytail and brushed her teeth, acutely aware that Todd could be just outside her door. The night's sleep had been better and longer than any in recent memory . Not wanting to evaluate the reasons why —afraid it might be that Todd slept in a room just fifty feet away—she embraced the foggy morning feeling.

Satisfied she no longer looked like a bum, Chrissy emerged from her room just as Todd was closing the door to their suite and rolling a cart into the space. "Good morning, sleepy head. I figured you'd be up soon, so I ordered us some breakfast."

"Coffee," was all that Chrissy could manage. She was used to being awake and putting on a cheery face pretty early in the morning at the cafe. That cheery face didn't usually show up until she was at least one cup of coffee in, which most people didn't realize. Once, they'd run out of coffee filters at the cafe. She'd nearly cried until her father went back to their house and got some from their personal stash.

Todd laughed at her surliness and poured her a cup. He added two creams and a sugar before handing it to her. "Be careful, it's hot." Chrissy inhaled the rich aroma and sighed. She could get used to this. Not only had someone else made the coffee, but Todd knew exactly how she liked it. He lifted the silver lids and rearranged the food so that each plate had pancakes, eggs and bacon. He removed the plastic wrap that was covering a small bowl of fresh cut fruit, then poured a cup of coffee for himself.

With a glance at her, he replaced the silver lid on one of the plates and grabbed the syrup and a fork for himself before sitting at the dining table across from her. They sat in comfortable silence as Chrissy slowly sipped her coffee and Todd ate his breakfast. Quiet sounds of silverware on glass and her exhalations as she blew on her coffee to cool it down were all that interrupted the peaceful morning.

Todd seemed content to let her sit and wake up at her own pace, which she appreciated. She neared the bottom of her cup of coffee and went to get a refill. "How did you sleep, Todd?"

He took a quick swallow of coffee before responding. "Not too bad. Beds were comfortable. How about you?"

"I slept like the dead. I didn't even realize how tired I was."

"Probably all that skating we did." Todd offered the suggestion with a shrug.

Chrissy just nodded. She knew there was more to it than that. She normally didn't sleep well at home—something about being alone in her little apartment. But she had refused to move back in with her parents. In her mind, she saw them too much at the cafe already. At least, she did until they moved. Last night was the first uninterrupted night of sleep she'd gotten in years, at least without the aid of one of the sleeping pills the doctor had given her. Even years later, she woke up breathless each night and reached for the comfort of her Bible. Until last night.

AFTER BREAKFAST, they decided to stay in and watch a couple of movies before going to Christmas Eve service. Todd logged into Netflix from the hotel TV and they settled in, agreeing that Chrissy could pick the first movie as long as Todd could pick the second. Todd sat sprawled out in one corner of the couch and propped up his feet, much like he had the day before when they arrived. Chrissy claimed one of the armchairs and put her feet on the matching ottoman. She quickly retrieved a throw blanket from the arm of the couch and cuddled up with it.

With a gleeful smile, Chrissy chose a Hallmark Christmas movie that she hadn't seen yet. Then, she watched out the corner of her eye for Todd's eyerolls and scoffs during the most predictable and cheesy parts of the movie. Thankfully, Todd chose a popular superhero film to watch next. Before they started it,

Todd ran across the street to grab sandwiches for lunch.

About halfway through the movie, Chrissy looked over at Todd and noticed he had fallen asleep. She slowly turned down the volume on the movie and continued watching it before succumbing to sleep herself.

When she woke up, the room was dim as the natural daylight had started to disappear into sunset. She glanced toward Todd and saw the couch was empty. There was light under the bathroom door and the steady drumming of the shower could be heard over the quiet hum of the fan. Checking her phone, she realized it was nearly time for dinner and church. Throwing off the blanket, Chrissy went to her room to change out of her pajamas.

While Chrissy was showering, Todd scoped out nearby churches for Christmas Eve services. By the time they were ready to go, they didn't have much time to grab dinner and make it to the church. They ordered at the counter of a small burger chain. They grabbed a booth and ate their burgers and shared an order of French fries. Chrissy was surprised there were places open and quite a few people out and about on Christmas Eve.

After they finished, they walked to the church,

passing people with their heads down against the cold wind. The "Windy City" was certainly living up to its name, all the tall buildings turning the streets and sidewalks into wind tunnels. The church was a few blocks away and they made it with little time to spare. It was dark by then, and the church was only dimly lit with candles and twinkling lights. A Nativity scene was displayed in the narrow strip of grass that separated the sidewalk from the building. Chrissy brushed her gloved hand on Todd's coat and commented quietly that it was nowhere near as nice as the one he made for the church in Minden. Again, she regretted not being in Minden at the Christmas Eve service. On the other hand, she was enjoying this trip with Todd so far. She knew herself well enough to admit she wouldn't have forgiven him yet if she hadn't been desperate for someone to come with her to Chicago.

They walked up the wide stone steps and entered the church through a door nearly twelve feel tall, peaked at the top and intricately carved. They were quietly handed a candle holder each, along with a program and a whispered "Merry Christmas." Inside, the church was stunning. Though it was dark, Chrissy could see large stained-glass windows lining the walls and an intricate alter standing at the far end of the sanctuary. The ceilings soared above them and though everyone was being quiet and respectful, the hushed voices carried through the huge space before echoing back to them. Todd placed his hand at the small of her back and gestured with his unlit candle to a pew about halfway up the aisle. As they sat, Chrissy watched an older woman light her candle using a larger candle attached to the pew on the aisle. Many others also had their candles lit, and she whispered to Todd, "Do you want to light your candle?"

Todd looked where she pointed at someone else lighting theirs and he quickly lit his candle. Then, Todd held his out to her so Chrissy could use his flame to light her own. The glow of the candlelight revealed his face in flickering orange and yellow light. She considered the man sitting next to her. When she was with Todd, Chrissy felt safe and confident. She felt beautiful and wanted. Remembering the kisses they had shared, her gaze dropped to his lips and the shadows cast across his face in the warm light. Todd was incredibly handsome, with a strong jawline under his beard and a charming smile. She'd always thought so, but in the last few months it had become increasingly difficult for her to ignore. Probably because of his thoughtful gestures and willingness to help. That kind of attention and flattery was addictive, and Chrissy wasn't sure she wanted to ignore or resist his advances any longer.

The piano playing softly in the background faded, and a worship leader invited everyone to stand and pray. Chrissy was quickly torn from her musings of Todd and lost in the age-old tradition of Christmas carols sung by candlelight. She quietly wiped a tear from her eye as the words to "Mary, Did You Know?" surrounded her. Todd's deep baritone rang in her ear and she moved closer. Todd slipped his arm around her waist and they stood together holding their candles, worshiping along with the room full of strangers, accompanied by only a piano and acoustic guitar. The simplicity of the worship session was fitting for the atmosphere in the church—reverent, yet joyful. The miracle of Christ's birth and the humble beginning of God on Earth as man. It was remarkable, and again, Chrissy was reminded of the incredible sacrifice her God had made on her behalf.

TODD SOAKED in the feeling of contentment during the service—his arm around Chrissy and the warm sound of worship with a group of believers. Christmas was his favorite holiday, ever since he accepted Christ and realized its profound significance. He held his small candle and watched the wax slowly drip down the edge before being caught in the little plastic shield. The pastor preached a simple message, highlighting the gift of Jesus given to the world. Todd was reminded that no matter what else he was or wasn't given in this life, he had been given Jesus and that was enough.

It needed to be enough.

As much as he wanted Chrissy and a family and perfect family Christmases of the future, there was no guarantee he would get it. But he had Jesus. And wasn't that amazing?

The final song—"Joy to the World"—was sung with an up-tempo beat, emphasizing the pastor's message that Jesus was a gift to the entire world and cause for a celebration beyond all others. Todd sang the words with a wide smile, as did Chrissy standing to his left while he held her to his side. No, there may not be a guarantee that Chrissy would be his forever. But, it wasn't going to stop him from praying and working to make it happen.

They walked back to the hotel in comfortable silence. Chrissy had her hand tucked in the crook of his elbow, much like the night they walked around Minden and looked at the Nativity. Their warm breath made clouds in front of them, visible in the cold night. But neither seemed in a big hurry as they strolled back to the hotel slowly, despite the cold and the late hour. Light snow was falling from the sky, but there was nothing on the ground yet. There weren't as many people on the street now and fewer cars. Street lights and Christmas lights in store windows illuminated the path, and the reflection of green and red shined on the damp streets from the traffic signals.

As they reached the hotel, Todd reluctantly pulled his arm from hers. Once in the elevator, he spoke. "This was a really great Christmas Eve, Christine."

Chrissy nodded and looked up at him. Her nose and cheeks were red from the cold and he couldn't help it; he pulled her close and gave her a soft kiss that ended when the elevator doors opened to their floor. Once inside their hotel suite, he released her fingers from his and said nothing but a simple "Good night," which she echoed. Todd watched her as Chrissy made her way across the living room and into her room before he turned and retreated to his.

21

*C*hrissy slept wonderfully again that night and woke up on Christmas morning with a smile on her face. The Christmas Eve service had been exactly what she needed, and experiencing it with Todd felt surprisingly appropriate. She went out to the living room to find coffee already sitting in a carafe on the counter, waiting to be poured. This morning, there was a small tray of bagels with cream cheese and fresh cut fruit. She fixed herself a cup of coffee and enjoyed the quiet morning, briefly wondering where Todd was. About halfway through her first mug, Todd came out of his room, still in sweatpants and a t-shirt and carrying a thin paper-sized package haphazardly wrapped in cheery paper and topped with a bow.

Chrissy suddenly realized that Todd had a Christmas present for her and that she had not even considered giving him something. The hotel room and the trip were already too much, but he cut off her stammering.

"It's nothing huge, I promise. I wanted to get you something. Besides, I ordered it before we were coming here." He pleaded with her, "Just open it?"

At the look in his eyes, she relented. Plus, Chrissy loved opening gifts. It *was* Christmas. Her guilt about not getting anything for Todd remained, however. He handed her the lightweight package and went to pour himself a cup of coffee and get a bagel. Chrissy unwrapped the holiday paper, smiling at the crumpled edges and excess tape. Inside was a manila folder with several printed sheets of paper, the first page revealed a diamond-shaped logo with fancy script declaring "B&J's Bistro". She flipped to the next page which contained smaller logos and alternate colors. The designs were incredible and Chrissy looked at Todd with questions in her eyes. He was leaning against the counter watching her with crossed ankles.

Todd shrugged. "One of the people I've been working on projects with for school freelances as a graphic designer. I asked him to work up some logo ideas for you. It's no big deal."

Chrissy stood up and walked over to him. "It's a very big deal, Todd Flynn." Instead of saying all the things her heart was screaming, she simply leaned into him and pressed her lips to his. Her hand rested on his chest as she pulled away. "This is the most thoughtful Christmas gift I have ever been given. Thank you." She leaned in and kissed his cheek before turning back toward the table.

Todd cleared his throat and uncrossed his ankles as he stood up. "I'm glad you like it. Merry Christmas, Chris."

"I'm sorry I didn't get you anything."

Todd waved her off. "I don't need anything, seriously."

Chrissy nodded, still unsure. "We'll see about that." She was determined to give him the best gift ever, even if it was after New Year's when he received it.

The city was quiet and snow fell softly outside the windows of their suite. They watched a Christmas movie on cable and enjoyed the morning together. Chinese food was their best option for takeout on the holiday, most restaurants being closed. Chinese food was hard to come by near Minden, but

Chrissy loved it. The Chinese place delivered to the hotel, and Chrissy's eyes grew wide when Todd entered the room with a huge brown takeout bag. It was way too much food, but leftovers for dinner would be perfect.

After lunch, Chrissy went to read and take a nap in her room. When she emerged an hour later, unable to sleep, she grabbed the remote in the empty living room. She turned on Netflix before walking over to the kitchen to grab a bottle of water. While she was in the kitchen, Todd came out of his bathroom, freshly showered and rubbing his hair with a towel. He wore jeans, but the sight of the tan, muscled chest caught Chrissy off guard. He froze when he saw her standing near the table staring at him—a mere five feet away.

"Let me just... I forgot my shirt in my bedroom." Todd was holding the towel to his hair in one hand and his discarded pajama pants in the other. The hint of a tattoo peeked out under the towel hanging over his shoulder. He turned toward his bedroom.

"Wait," Chrissy's word surprised even her. With a boldness she didn't recognize, she crossed the space and brushed the towel aside, her fingers cold and slightly damp from the condensation on the water bottle she held. Todd held his breath as she lightly traced the tattoo. It was a simple drawing of a lantern, three inches across, with the words "Isaiah 42:16" written in script below it. Chrissy looked to him for the answer to her unspoken question.

With a rough voice, Todd recited, "I will turn the darkness into light before them and make the rough places smooth. These are the things I will do; I will not forsake them." Dropping the towel, he shifted her fingers to the top of the lantern, where the skin was raised and bumpy beneath the ink. A scar. "This is where my dad burned me with his cigarette when I was nine. He found me hiding books from the library under my bed."

Chrissy's eyes were torn from her hand resting on his chest to meet his as he gazed down at her. There was no bitterness in his voice or on his face. She didn't know what to say. How had Todd become such a good man with that as his example? How had he moved beyond the terrible hurt inflicted by someone who was supposed to love him? "That's awful," she shakily replied after a moment. Todd's fingers released hers and she instinctively flattened her palm against his warm skin. She looked at her fingers again as they seemed to move without permission, sliding down from the tattoo toward his waist. Her flattened palm lifting until only her fingertips brushed his defined abs. Just as the texture under her fingers changed from warm skin to the rough denim of his jeans, Todd grabbed her wrist.

He leaned down and kissed her firmly, just barely nipping her lower lip between his teeth before soothing the spot again with his tongue. Releasing her wrist, Todd stepped back with purpose. "I'll be right back." He reached down for the towel, pooled in a heap near his feet, and retreated to his bedroom.

Chrissy let out a shaky breath and lifted two fingers to her bottom lip where the memory of his teeth and lips on hers still tingled.

TODD COLLAPSED BACKWARD onto his bed, staring at the ceiling and reliving the past five minutes. He never expected Chrissy to be awake. Why had he shared the story behind his tattoo? The last thing he wanted was Chrissy's pity. His dad was a jerk. Big deal. Todd knew God had made the rough places smooth, easing the pain from his past. And slowly, the darkness was turning to light.

With a growl, Todd rubbed his face with the towel. It was unwise to be in this hotel room with Chrissy. When she touched him, everything else disappeared. It was, without a doubt, a recipe for disaster. The desire to walk back to the living room and deepen their kiss was nearly overwhelming.

Grabbing his shirt, he quickly put it on, then he said a quick prayer for strength and wisdom. He heard God's response before he even finished, reminding him to flee temptation. Todd rubbed a hand down his face. *Where can I go?* The luxurious hotel room that seemed so expansive upon check-in was suddenly far too small. Todd slid his roomkey in his pocket and kept his distance from Chrissy as he left the hotel room.

Todd sat in the lobby skimming magazines and then explored, peering into empty ballrooms. An hour later, he had exhausted the nervous energy created in the tense moments in the kitchenette. During a stop at the front desk he received a hearty "Merry Christmas, sir" and a few boardgames to take with him to the suite.

TODD DISAPPEARED and Chrissy paced the suite for an hour, fretting about how she had crossed the line and also worrying about what would happen tomorrow. They would go to the bank first thing in the morning and she would plead her case to Mr. Cochran. Hopefully, the revenue statements for the last several months and the estimate for repairs would be sufficient. Plus, Chrissy had printed out her mock-up of the new menu for the bistro.

Todd's return to the suite immediately filled her with a sense of relief. She didn't want to examine her body's physical response to his presence. How could someone simultaneously tie her up in knots and bring her such peace? With unspoken agreement, they ignored 'the tattoo incident', as she was coming to think of it. Instead, they played board games and Christmas movies on cable. Todd's company helped keep Chrissy's mind off what would happen the next day. Despite her preparations, she tossed and turned restlessly, worrying about the meeting and praying it would go well.

Chrissy spent extra time in the morning reading her favorite verse, but they didn't really help as much as she hoped. When she heard Todd answer the door for room service, she welcomed the distraction and went out to get coffee.

Todd's warm voice greeted her, "Good morning, beautiful."

Chrissy blushed at the compliment and realized that she hadn't even brushed her hair before coming out. She tried to tame it nonchalantly with her fingers and was grateful that she at least hadn't slept on wet hair this time. "Morning."

As she drank her coffee, Todd raised his eyebrows at her. At her confused look, he moved his gaze to her leg, bouncing up and down of its own accords shaking the entire dining table. Chrissy immediately stopped and concentrated on her coffee. Before long, the *ting-ting-ting* of her fingernails on the ceramic mug rang out as she drummed an impatient pattern near the handle. She pulled her hand away and looked up at Todd to see if he had noticed. He chuckled andshook his head. "A little anxious this morning, are we?"

"Well yeah!" Chrissy released the pent-up energy and anxiety she had been feeling all night. "Today will make or break everything. What if he says no? What if they laugh at me?" Then softer, "What if they say yes?"

Todd laughed and set his coffee on the table. He opened his arms and waved her in. "Come here," when she just looked at him, he repeated, "Come here."

Chrissy reluctantly obeyed and sat on his lap as he wrapped his arms around her. She laid her head on his shoulder and immediately nuzzled to get closer. Todd stroked her back and began to speak. "You've got this, Christine Mathes. You are amazing and brave and no matter what happens at the bank today, I am so proud of you. If they can't see what an amazing thing you are doing, it is their loss. God has a plan for you and for the cafe, Chris. Just relax. Take a deep breath. In and out. Good girl." Chrissy soaked in the encouragement and took another deep breath. "Father, calm Chrissy's spirit today. Give her a spirit of boldness and confidence, not one of fear and anxiety. Stand beside her and remind her of Your presence throughout the meeting. Give her peace, regardless of the outcome. And Father? Show me how to support her the best way I can. Thank you for your promise to work all things for good and thank you for this friendship and for your presence in our lives. Amen."

With that prayer, all the anxiety Chris had been feeling and had been unable to banish on her own was gone. Silent tears ran down her cheek and she discretely tried to wipe them on his white shirt. A snotty sniffle gave her away and Todd laughed. The sound rumbled beneath her as his shoulders shook slightly. "You're going to be just fine, Chris. Do you trust me?" At her nod, he continued. "Do you trust God?"

Chrissy nodded once more and sat up. "Thanks, Todd. That was just what I needed."

Todd removed his arms from around her and drawled in an exaggerated southern accent. "Darlin', you can sit on my lap and cry anytime you need to."

She playfully slapped his damp shoulder and got up to return to her side of the table, feeling a hundred times more confident about the meeting.

When they arrived at the bank, Todd took a seat in one of the over-sized armchairs and waited while Chrissy approached the banking desk. The clerk disappeared for a moment and then returned, shaking her head a couple of times as Chrissy talked. Chrissy turned back toward him with her file of papers and a frustrated expression. Todd hurried to his feet, grabbing her bag. He could tell she was upset so he ushered her out of the building before she started to cry. Unsure of what had happened, he knew there was no way she'd even had time to plead her case about the loan. They found a place to sit on a concrete retaining wall near some stairs at the front of the bank and Todd waited. He kept an arm around her and rubbed her upper arm beneath her coat.

Finally, Chrissy pulled herself together enough to explain. "I said I was there to meet with the loan officer, but apparently they aren't in today! Our appointment is for tomorrow. I feel like such an idiot. We could have stayed in Minden for Christmas and been totally fine for the appointment. And now I have to come back tomorrow! Ugh! And I was so ready, you know. After your pep talk this morning and everything, I really felt like I was going to walk in there and knock their socks off."

Todd considered this. "Well, you'll just have to do the same thing tomorrow instead. I'm sure I can whip up another pep talk. And besides, this means we get another day in the city together. We'll just do something fun." Chrissy didn't seem convinced, but Todd ignored her and pulled out his phone. He called the hotel and added an extra night to their reservation, relieved there was no issue. They'd planned on returning to the hotel after her meeting and checking out, but now he began thinking of things to do. An architectural boat tour was highly recommended, but it was cold and he didn't even know if they operated in the winter. He remembered some of the other museums and attractions he'd come across researching for the trip.

Grabbing Chrissy's files, he stuffed them in her bag and took her hand. "Come on, Chris. We might as well go have some fun while we are here." He flagged down a cab and opened the door for Chris to enter before him, not giving her further chance to protest.

odd directed the cab to the Museum of Science and Industry and they spent the day exploring exhibits on coal mines, energy, and submarines. Chrissy stayed grumpy, despite Todd's best efforts to cheer her up. She stewed about the appointment, and Todd's cheerful demeanor just made it worse. He added tidbits of information to what was explained in the videos and placards across the museum, and Chrissy was reminded that the guy she had known for so long wasn't even the man standing next to her.

Todd smiled as a pair of young kids with their parents cut in front of them, running from one hands-on display to another. The longer the day went on, though, the more Chrissy withdrew from him. She—overachiever and straight-A student—couldn't even remember the date for the appointment at the bank correctly. Todd, on the other hand, apparently knew random information about everything from submarines to genetic engineering of farm animals. The entire day at the museum was one big wake-up call—Todd was out of her league. Chrissy snapped out sarcastic remarks when he tried to compliment her in the mirror maze, then ignored the confused and wounded look on his face.

Sensing her mood, Todd asked if she was ready to leave. But Chrissy insisted she was fine to stay and continue exploring. When they left, it was nearly dark and Todd tried to cajole Chrissy into giving an opinion for dinner, but she wouldn't say much. He found a restaurant a few blocks from their hotel, and they took another cab back.

Todd gave the host their name and they were seated within a few minutes. The food was good, but the conversation was stilted, unlike it had ever been with them before. At least the TVs scattered throughout the space gave him an excuse to let Chrissy sit in silence. Even the waiter seemed to notice the tension between them and dropped off their food and check without saying much at all. Frustrated, Todd slipped cash into the folder and tossed it back on the table before walking out of the restaurant with an irritated glance at Chrissy. Once outside, he confronted her.

Todd rubbed his beard and his eyes flashed in the light of the street lamp. "Chrissy, what is your deal? Was today so terrible that you need to mope around? You've been snarky and upset all day!" Then, his tone softened. "I know you're disappointed about the appointment this morning, but it's happening tomorrow instead. What's the big deal?"

His anger she could handle, but his understanding and grace needled her. Chrissy whirled around and snapped at him. "Just leave me alone, Todd! I don't need you to make everything better. You can't fix it!" She knew she'd been awful to him all day. And now, when he was finally fed up enough to call her out on her behavior, Chrissy lashed out at him as though she were the one with a right to be upset. In reality, he was the one who should be walking away from her. Chrissy stormed off in the opposite direction, not sure where she was going. She just knew she couldn't look at the hurt in his eyes from her outburst.

Night had fallen in Chicago, and Chrissy dodged a few other people on the sidewalk, trying to wipe the tears from her face before they froze in the chill of the night. Remnants of snow still lined the sidewalks near the curb and the edge of the building. She rushed for a few blocks before slowing down. Despite her hands tucked in her pockets, the cold seeped in now that she wasn't power walking or jogging. Glancing at the buildings to get her bearings, Chrissy realized she didn't even know where their hotel was. Laughter erupted from a group of men across the street and she felt her pulse kick into overdrive. Chrissy spun in a circle a couple of times, looking at the street names.

None of them looked familiar.

The sound of a car horn from the intersection to her left made her jump. Her breathing grew shallower and Chrissy squeezed her eyes shut, trying to block out the noise and calm her racing thoughts. Suddenly, a male voice came from her right. "Are you okay, lady?" The voice was relatively quiet and would have sounded concerned and friendly to anyone passing by.

That was all it took for the spiral of panic to take her under. Chrissy's eyes flew open as her chest seized up. The man who spoke was sitting on a bench with a middle-aged woman. Rationally, Chrissy knew he wasn't a threat, but her body couldn't process that signal. She couldn't breathe, couldn't speak. Her heart was racing in her chest and she shook uncontrollably. Icy hands grabbed at her chest as it squeezed painfully with the lack of air. The sounds of the city and the stranger asking about her well-being seemed strangely distant before everything faded.

The next thing Chrissy knew, she was looking up into Todd's concerned eyes. The cold from the cement where she sat was wicking through her dress pants. The couple who'd been talking to her when the panic attack hit was standing and watching with troubled expressions on their faces. Todd was talking to her and slowly she focused in on his words.

"...you okay? Can you hear me? Chrissy, what happened?"

Chrissy waved him off and started to get up from her uncomfortable place on the ground. Todd quickly shouldered most of her weight and led her to the vacated bench. She dropped her head between her knees and rubbed her back while muttering reassurances. "It's okay. You're okay now. Just breathe." He whispered prayers as well, a soft murmur above the noise of the traffic and pedestrians as life went on around them.

They sat there for a few minutes until Chrissy finally sat up and looked around again. The man and woman were still there, watching. "Are you okay, sweetie?" the woman asked in a quiet voice. "Do you know this man? I think he was following you."

Chrissy tried her best to smile at the kind woman, "I'm okay. And yes. This is my... friend, Todd." She desperately wanted to say 'boyfriend', but she knew she needed to tell him her secret before she could do that. Would he even still want her after she treated him so horribly today?

"Chris, what happened? One minute you were fine, and then I see you grab your chest and hit the deck. Do I need to call a doctor?" She could see Todd fighting back a hundred other questions in an effort not to overwhelm her.

"I'll tell you about it when we get back to the hotel. Can you just take me back, please?" She could breathe again and was no longer dizzy, but she felt incredibly weak and small. Chrissy felt like she'd been hit by a truck, and being out on the street in the dark still made her feel anxious in the aftermath of the panic attack. Despite the absence of any real threat, Chrissy knew the overwhelming anxiety would take a few hours to disappear.

～

INSTEAD OF WALKING the nearly eight blocks back to the hotel, Todd flagged down a cab and helped Chrissy in. To his surprise, Chrissy sat in the middle seat and rested against his shoulder. His eyes never left her face during the ride; she was nearly asleep with her eyes closed the entire time. Not that he minded at all. Would she let him support her once this episode was behind them? The cab dropped them off under the canopy at the hotel and they made their way to the room in silence, Todd's arm still around her shoulders. When they got to the room, Todd settled her in one corner of the couch and gave her a soft throw blanket from the arm chair. A few minutes later, he brought a mug with a tea bag floating in it. "Here. Drink this."

Todd sat on the other side of the couch and wrung his hand, still unsure that Chrissy was okay. She seemed detached and it worried him. Worse, he didn't know how to help. He'd gotten her the tea because that seemed like something Miss Ruth would do if someone was upset at her house. As much as he wanted to shake Chrissy and yell at her for taking off, he also wanted to do nothing more than pull her close to him and hold her for the rest of the night. It was a frustrating mix of emotions.

While he bit his tongue and waited for her to talk

to him, he prayed. He prayed for patience and understanding. He petitioned God on behalf of Chrissy's health. Lastly, he prayed for their relationship and whatever the fight had been about. Just when he was about to cycle back to praying for patience, Chrissy began to speak.

She stared at the mug in her hands, instead of at him. "I'm sorry about today."

As soon as she started, Todd tried to interject. He didn't care about the museum; he needed to know what happened tonight.

Weakly, Chrissy held up a hand to cut off his objections. "I'm sorry about today. I was upset about the bank and I took it out on you. You've been nothing but amazing to me as long as we've been friends. At the museum today, I realized again just how smart and accomplished you are. What an amazing guy you are, and I felt—I feel," she corrected, "so undeserving of you." Again, he tried to object and she silenced him with a look. "It was really stupid of me to run off outside the restaurant. It could have been so much worse." Chrissy fell silent for a moment. After she took a deep breath, she continued. "You know I lived here when I went to school. But you don't know why I came home.

Nobody really does, even my parents only know pieces of it.

"During the fall semester of my sophomore year, I was walking home from a late-night study session. Instead of taking a cab, I walked alone. It was stupid and naive of me."

Todd's heart began to sink as he listened to her story, afraid he knew where it was going.

Chrissy continued with a shaky voice. "Three guys. They started talking to me outside a bar. When I... When I tried to ignore them, they got angry."

Todd moved closer on the couch, unable to stop himself from trying to touch her. She retreated further into the corner of the couch, curling into a ball. He stopped his movement toward her despite every muscle in his body aching to be close to her. "Just let me finish, please?" she pleaded.

Staring once more at her tea, she fiddled with the teabag and kept talking. "They forced me... into the alley and," she swallowed and shook her head, unable to speak the rest of the sentence. Tears fell from where they had pooled on her eyelashes. As though she was unable to stop the floodgates now that she had opened them, she went on. Todd swore he felt his heart actually break for her pain. Chrissy squeezed her eyes shut and let it out. "They ripped my clothes and said horrible things to me. And even though I prayed before the attack and fought back until I couldn't..." She trailed off. Looking into her tea again, she continued. "I thought they were going to kill me. Afterward, I actually wished they had. If I had only walked with my friends..."

Todd cut her off abruptly. "It was *not* your fault, Chris." She shook her head, seeming to disagree with him. "No," he insisted. "They are monsters and nothing you did brought it on." He was agitated that she didn't believe him and his stomach ached at the thought of her enduring something so terrible. "It makes me sick that this happened to you. Chrissy, you are beautiful and perfect and loved. Do you realize that?" She sniffed and kept crying.

"I've been so hypocritical, angry at you for keeping your secret when I've been keeping one for years as well. I'm not the girl you thought I was either. I barely sleep at night, I failed out of college because I couldn't get out of bed to go to class. Usually, I can put on a cheery face every day at the diner, and I'm generally a happy person. But I'm still broken! I was so angry with God for letting this happen to me. Sometimes I still am."

Todd was right next to her now, and he took the mug from her hands, lacing her fingers with his.

"Christine Elise Mathes. I don't know why God lets bad things happen to us." He held her hand over his heart where the tattoo laid under his sweater. "I do know that He turns darkness into light. And I know that nothing you've told me tonight makes me think any less of you. If anything, I'm even more amazed at your strength and resilience. I wish it hadn't taken a scare you had tonight for you to confide in me, but you know I understand keeping secrets, too."

Todd took a deep breath before admitting what he'd wanted to for weeks. "Chris, I love you. You. Exactly as you are. This trip with you has been the best few days of my entire life. But if you can't get past who I am—a guy who loves to learn and who hoards books—then I need to know. I'm done keeping secrets from the world. I'm done keeping secrets from you."

Chrissy was silent for a moment, feeling his heart beat under her hand. Todd's heart sank as the moment dragged on. This was it. The end. He'd finally let everything out in the open and she couldn't accept it. Then, she lifted her gaze from where it rested on his chest and looked into his eyes. Hers were smiling, though still rimmed with red and watery. "I love you, too."

And with that admission, Todd pulled her close

and held her tightly, determined to never let go. His heart lifted a silent prayer. *Thank you, God. Thank you!* Then, he remembered that he had one secret left to tell and pulled Chrissy away from him slightly. "Ummm, there is one more thing that you should know."

Todd looked embarrassed and Chrissy raised an eyebrow. "No more secrets, huh?"

"Yeah, this is the last one. I inherited some money when my dad died. Like, kind of a lot of money," he admitted.

Chrissy just smiled. "Well, I'm glad you haven't taken on thousands of dollars in debt for this trip. That wouldn't be a very good start to a marriage."

Todd coughed. "A marriage?"

Chrissy blushed, "I mean, if we...Once we've dated..." She was flustered and smiling and Todd absolutely loved it. He loved the sound of marriage, too. He was going to do it right, though—a ring and bended knee and all that. Silencing her rambling thoughts, he pulled her close and covered her lips with his.

23

*T*he next morning, they went back to the bank. Chrissy didn't even need a pep talk; she was still on cloud nine from the magic of the evening before. They had stayed up late, kissing and cuddling and talking until they both were fighting chronic yawns. The feelings of contentedness followed her all morning and accompanied her as she walked confidently to the bank clerk and explained that she had an appointment with Dennis Cochran, the loan officer. She was quickly shown to a small office visible from the main lobby. The name on the door read Lloyd Parley, and for the first time that morning, Chrissy started to worry.

She put on a brave face and introduced herself to

the portly middle-aged man at the desk. He half-heartedly lifted his lower half from the chair as he shook her hand and then immediately sat down again. He gestured to the empty chair on her side of the large wooden desk.

"Good morning, Miss..." he trailed off, waiting for her name.

"Mathes," she supplied. "From Bud and Janine's Cafe in Minden, Indiana."

"Ah yes, of course. Let me just pull up your accounts with us." He turned to the computer off to his right.

In the silence, Christine ventured the question. "Excuse me, Mr. Parley. I was led to believe I had a meeting with Dennis Cochran? My father said he has previously handled all our accounts."

The serious man across from her just waved a hand. "Dennis retired about eight months ago, and I took over all his accounts." Then he lightly chuckled. "It's a good thing, too. He was far too sentimental and didn't make the best decisions for the bank, in my opinion." He clicked a few more things on the computer and his eyes flitted across the screen briefly. "Ah, there we go. Bud and Janine's Cafe. The account has been open since 1971. Looks like there are still about ten years remaining to pay on the mortgage, due to the refinance from five years ago. And you, Miss Mathes, were added as an owner on the account about four years ago."

Chrissy didn't know anything about the refinance, but she did know that the building wasn't theirs outright. She was surprised that she had been an owner in the business for that long, but it didn't really matter right now.

He didn't say anything else, so she took her opportunity to explain. "Yes, sir, that's me. I'm here to request a loan. Now that my parents have moved on, I'd like to do some fairly significant renovations to the cafe. I plan to re-open with a new menu, a newly designed space, and an updated approach to marketing and overall direction for the restaurant." She began pulling out the documents she'd brought along.

"Let me stop you right there. Looking at your balance statements from the last several months, I can see that the cafe is barely scraping by," he said, wrinkling his brow in disgust.

Chrissy nodded. "I know, that's why..."

Mr. Parley went on, as though she hadn't spoken. "We here at First Presidential Bank don't believe that the outlook for a business in your small town is very good. Especially with the added monthly expense of loan repayment on top of the existing mortgage. There just isn't enough business to warrant further investment on behalf of the bank."

"But sir, just look at the changes I'm going to..."

"I don't need to see the changes to know that it isn't going to work. Minden isn't where we want to extend our capital. Thank you for coming in today." As an afterthought and with total lack of sincerity, he added, "We appreciate your business." He turned back to his computer and closed out of the windows. His dismissal was complete and left no room for further argument.

Her mouth opened and closed, like a fish gasping for water. When she couldn't find the words, Chrissy gathered her papers quickly and tore out of the room. She caught Todd's eye where he waited, flipping through a magazine, and then proceeded to walk back out of the bank for the second time in as many days. She was livid. How dare he just dismiss her without even hearing her out? *The bank's money is too good for Minden? Well, Minden is too good for them.* She began thinking of where she could move the business accounts so she never had to deal with the insufferable ego of the banker sitting in the building behind her.

Todd caught up with her and tugged her arm to get her to stop and look at him. He didn't ask the question but gave Chrissy the opening to tell him what had happened. She took the opportunity and vented, starting from the beginning. "Dennis Cochran doesn't even work there anymore. During the phone call and the time yesterday and even when I got here this morning, they just let me believe I would be meeting with him. And then they ambush me with Mr. Sentimental-decision-making-is-bad instead. Can you believe he said that the 'outlook wasn't good' for a business in Minden?" She made little quotation marks with her fingers and spat the words out. "He didn't even look at the new business plan or the renovations. He just completely wrote me off and sent me on my way with a pat on the head. He even said 'we appreciate your business'. Ugh, the nerve of that guy. I'm moving all the accounts to another bank. He treated me with no respect at all."

Todd listened patiently and when she had run out of steam, he pulled her in for a hug. Chrissy buried her face in his coat and the anger evaporated into despair. She started to cry, sick of how much she'd done so in the past few weeks. "I'm sorry, Chris. He's an idiot if he didn't even take the time to see what you have planned. And he definitely doesn't know Minden if he thinks you won't make it. The cafe, all of Main Street really, is the pin that holds our little community together. No one is going to let you disappear into the woodwork."

She lifted her head and sniffed. "I need to think about what to do next. I had so much hope this loan would be the answer for me to make the bistro happen."

Todd nodded, understanding her need to process. "You'll have plenty of time to consider what comes next. But first, let's go do something to cheer you up a bit before we head back home. Okay?"

Chrissy nodded gratefully.

"And Chris? Just don't forget that true hope doesn't lie in banks or any specific outcome of a situation, despite our tendency to focus on those things. Our hope comes from the Lord, like it says in Psalms. He has something amazing planned for you and, I honestly believe, for the restaurant, too."

THEY JUMPED in a cab and Todd told the driver where to go. Chrissy could have sworn she heard him say "Italy", but if there was a 'Little Italy' neighborhood in Chicago, she'd never heard about it. Instead, they pulled up outside a modern looking building with "Eataly" displayed on the banner. It sounded like exactly her kind of place and she felt a surge of excitement.

When they stepped inside, Chrissy was immediately overwhelmed with the smells. She could identify fresh bread and chocolate, though she couldn't quite see it yet. There were multiple escalators leading to upper levels. It was almost like a shopping mall, and they quickly found a 'Directory' board with a map of the space. Different recommended "experiences" were offered: a wine-focused visit, a lunch rotation, a learning day filled with classes and demonstrations. Instead of choosing one, they decided to wander and see what would catch their eye.

One of the first little shops tucked into the large space served pastries and coffee, so they got espresso and a flaky layered pastry called *sfogliatella* to share. They sipped their drinks and walked through small shops and stands. There was an entire store dedicated to different types of olive oil and balsamic vinegar, and Chrissy got a gift set for Norm as thanks for running the kitchen while she was gone.

There were several small bakery shops. Some

focused on breads, some on cakes and desserts, and some on handmade pasta. They looked at the menus of half a dozen restaurants and watched expert chocolatiers create intricate truffles and cordials. Todd tapped her on the shoulder and reminded her they should choose a place for lunch before heading back to Minden. Chrissy considered the possibility of adding specialty flatbreads to her bistro menu while they shared a couple of lunch entrees. The only place to get something resembling pizza in Minden was the QuikStop and Chrissy didn't think that really counted.

She hadn't thought about the restaurant all morning until then, but the reminder that the bistro couldn't happen since she didn't get the loan brought her mood down quickly. Todd noticed her sudden attitude shift.

"What's wrong?"

"I was just thinking about the bistro. I can't believe I won't get to do all the things I dreamed of. And now, how will I pay you for everything you've done so far?"

Todd had something that would, hopefully, let Chrissy have everything she dreamed of. Him too, if all went according to plan. He wasn't ready yet, though. Instead, he touched her arm across the table and tried to reassure her. "We'll figure it out, Chris. It's going to be just fine."

Chrissy flashed him a tight smile in gratitude, but she didn't look convinced.

They drove back from Chicago and went straight to the cafe to check in. It was slow when they arrived, with the restaurant scheduled to close in about an hour. They exchanged a private smile when they found Ruth sitting at the counter, chatting and laughing with Norman, who leaned on the counter across from her with a grin. Since Norman had started, Ruth had been found much more frequently in the cafe. She, of course, claimed it was all because she happened to be in town making plans at the church or with the baker for the wedding. Nevertheless, it made Chrissy happy to see Ruth's youthful laughter and nearly flirtatious conversations with the recently hired chef. From their current postures, Norman had become equally enamored with Ruth in the few interactions they'd had. He straightened and smoothed his apron as they entered the restaurant and greeted the pair.

"Welcome back! How did it go?" Norm was as excited as Chrissy to make the transition to B&J Bistro.

"Thank you. Unfortunately, it didn't go as well as

expected, but I'm not giving up yet." Chrissy put on a brave face for her employee. Despite wracking her brain during the ride home from Chicago, she didn't have a solution.

Mandy left an hour ago, after the lunch crowd had cleared out. Chrissy made a mental note to call her later and thank her again for covering. She'd picked up a cool science kit for Mandy to use at the daycare during their trip to the Science and Industry Museum as a thank you gift. She pulled out the plain brown paper giftbag that held Norm's oil and vinegar set and gave it to him. Norm read the labels with enthusiasm, exclaiming loudly to Ruth that she "had to taste this one with a loaf of fresh bread". Chrissy's mood lifted at his reaction and his friendship with Ruth.

She asked Ruth about the wedding plans. It was only about a month away, and Chrissy knew from conversations with Charlotte that it couldn't come soon enough for them. Ruth chatted for a moment about the flowers and bemoaned the lack of a florist in Minden. With the January wedding date, Charlotte and Ruth had decided to embrace the season, so the wedding colors were a frosty blue and silver. There would be accents in the bouquets that gave the appearance of ice-covered greenery, and the centerpieces would have elements of evergreens in addition to snowflake motifs included on the programs and invitations. Ruth was clearly enjoying the process of planning this wedding, and was determined to give Charlotte the full bridal experience, despite the small wedding and short time frame.

Ruth jumped in, "Actually, I'm so glad you asked. I was just talking with Norman. Charlotte and I were talking and we really want to ask if you and Norman here would cater the wedding? Obviously, you know the date is set for January 27th, which is less than a month away. Do you think you'd be able to do it? We are expecting about fifty people."

Chrissy was shocked. She'd never considered catering as a part of her business, but quickly saw the opportunity it provided. She looked at Norman and held her hands open. "I think it's a great idea, but it is really up to you, Norm. I'll be busy being in the wedding as a bridesmaid, so the day of the event, the work will fall to you. Plus, I've got some other projects in the works for the cafe... So, Norm? Your call."

Norm quickly agreed and he and Ruth started talking about menu options and pricing.

Briefly, Chrissy's thoughts flashed to what her wedding would be like with Todd. She quickly pushed away the thought and admonished herself for getting ahead of things. It had been less than twenty-four hours since they cemented their relationship. Still, she couldn't help but picture him at the end of the aisle, waiting for her as she walked toward him holding her father's arm.

24

Todd quickly threw together a plan, enlisting the help of his friends. Anxiously, Todd convinced Charlotte to go with him to Indianapolis on Friday to buy a ring. With the overly friendly salesperson watching him, Todd studied the glittering rings and tried to imagine one on Chrissy's finger. Wanting to shower her with the best of everything, he pointed to one with a large center stone.

Charlotte slipped it on her own finger and shook her head. "Todd, Chrissy doesn't need the Hope Diamond on her hand to marry you. Think about Chrissy and look at the rings. Which one makes you think of her?" Chrissy slipped the ring off and handed it back to the saleswoman, who gave her a tight smile as she saw her commission slowly slipping away. Todd looked back in the case, moving away from the large, cold stones and toward something more practical and delicate for Christine. He found one and tapping a finger on the glass, pointed it out to Chrissy. This ring had an icy blue center stone, with several smaller diamonds and an intricate band that twisted around the setting. The blue of the ring reminded him of Chrissy's eyes, and when he said as much to Charlotte, he saw her eyes shimmer and she nodded. Even the regal saleswoman gave a genuine smile and pulled the ring out. It was perfect.

New Year's Eve was three days away and Todd was determined to make it a celebration to remember. The cafe typically closed at 4 pm on Sunday and Todd arranged for Chrissy to come out to his workshop immediately after closing, so Norm could get things set up at the cafe. Unbeknownst to Chrissy, there would be a New Year's Eve party at the bistro. When Sunday came around, Todd could barely contain himself through church. Knowing he had the ring in his pocket and sitting next to Chrissy, he fought the urge to drop to a knee right there. His pulse raced and his neck felt clammy from the nagging fear he would lay everything on the line and be rejected. Despite the closeness and conversations he and Chrissy had since their trip to Chicago, part of him still doubted he was good enough. Part of him still felt like the scared little boy hiding library books under the covers with a flashlight late at night. The other part of him was so eager to tie his life to Chrissy's forever that he was willing to make a fool of himself in front of the whole town to make it happen. But he waited. Their conversation needed to happen at his house, so he could tell her—and ask her—everything at once.

CHRISSY DEBATED for days what she could get Todd for Christmas. He'd given her so much: the trip, the logos, the work he was doing for the restaurant. She considered every option but it all seemed cliché or impersonal. After everything Todd had done for her, she wanted to give him something special. The desire to give him something to show she knew, and accepted, the real Todd Flynn, who watched documentaries and could talk about a random museum exhibit for twenty minutes, was overwhelming. But also, he was the same Todd Flynn who did love football and Jesus and had been her friend for twenty years. Todd Flynn was both of those people. What kind of gift could encompass that? With a flash of brilliance, Chrissy finally figured out the perfect thing and ordered it with two-day shipping. When Todd insisted she come out to his workshop on New Year's Eve after the cafe closed, Chrissy grabbed the gift to bring it with her.

Chrissy left Norm at the cafe, cleaning up a few remaining things from lunch and headed to Todd's.

When she arrived, he greeted her with a warm hug and a long kiss, "I'm glad you're here."

"I don't know what's so important, but I've got something for you first." Todd looked surprised and she smiled. "I know it is a little late, but I wanted to get you something special. After all the things you've given me, this seems small in comparison. Merry Christmas, Todd."

The two packages were wrapped separately and tied together with a ribbon, so Todd removed it and began unwrapping the smaller package. When he revealed the e-reader she had picked out for him, he got a huge smile on his face. She spoke up with an explanation. "Now that I know how much you love to read, I figured this would let you carry thousands of books with you anywhere. It includes an entire year subscription to the e-book lending library, too."

He turned the box over in his hands and his

mouth hung open. "Chris, I love it. I... I don't think I've ever received such a thoughtful gift before. Thank you."

"Now open the other one. It's cold out here."

With a smile at her bossy tone, Todd replied, "Yes, ma'am."

The second package was a beautiful coffee table book on woodworking, filled with pictures and some of the history and famous craftsmen of the past. It featured detailed explanations of different techniques and highlights of some of the most remarkable modern-day woodworkers and their art.

Chrissy spoke again. "I want you to know that I see all of you—the athlete, the craftsman, the book lover, and the business owner. I see you and I love you."

Todd didn't say anything right away, but pulled her into his arms and kissed the top of her forehead. "Oh, I love you, too."

"Come on, let me show you what I wanted you to see."

"Oh yeah, you wanted something," she teased. "What's so important that you needed to show me today?"

"Come on, and you'll see!" He took her hand and led her through the snowy gravel to the workshop.

There, he had arranged all the tables he had built in the large open space, as though it was the cafe. A beautiful hand-painted sign with the logo she'd chosen was hung from the rafter near the front door. A small mason jar sat on each table with a single rose in each. He let her enter and hung back to watch her explore.

She trailed her fingers across the top of a table. The reclaimed wood was beautiful, and the lacquer he had applied to make the tables easy to wipe down was the perfect functional touch. She counted the tables and looked back at him. "I don't understand; I don't have the money. I told you to stop building things for a while!"

Todd just smiled. "I know you don't have the money. But Chris... I do."

"I can't take your money, Todd." She looked away from him, embarrassed at his offer.

"I'm not asking you to take my money. Christine, I want to be your partner. In B&J's Bistro— and in life," he added.

With a gasp, she turned back to him sharply. Todd looked up at her now from where he knelt on the cold concrete floor of the shop. He held the ring and tried to convey the depth of his feelings with a look. At her expression of shock, he spoke again. "I love you, Christine Mathes. I think I have since elementary school. The more I get to know you, the more amazed I am at the woman you've become. I want to spend every Christmas with you from here on out. I want to tackle every impossible project with you by my side. If you feel even remotely the same, let me love you for eternity. I can't imagine life without you."

Chrissy shook her head in protest. "Todd, this is crazy. We haven't even dated!" She pulled him to his feet.

"If you think we need to date, we definitely can. But I already know you're the woman God chose for me." The next part was hard for him to say, but she needed to know that he believed in her and that she wasn't obligated to marry him just to make her dream come true at the restaurant. "And even if you aren't ready to say yes to being my wife, I want to invest in the bistro as a partner. The money I got when my dad died has been sitting there taunting me, and I can think of no better use for it than to invest in you —and in this town. Forget that big city banker; he doesn't know you and he doesn't know Minden. But I do. I know you, Chris, and you know me."

∽

CHRISSY CROSSED her arms and held herself together by her biceps. She desperately wanted to say yes. To everything. She wanted to embrace the picture he painted of Christmases together, of a partner in the bistro and in life. She considered the man in front of her and the gift he had been to her in the past few months. Their friendship spanned years before now, but she wasn't sure she could have survived the last two months without him. Even in their fight, Chrissy had the assurance of his confidence in her to lean on.

Chrissy considered her past and the secret she had kept from everyone for so long. How the shame and the hurt of her assault had colored her thoughts for years, telling the story that she was worthless and undesirable. How different that story was from the one her Creator had been trying to tell her. She was worthy of happiness; she was wonderfully made.

And the man in front of her wanted her.

Not the image of perfection he'd carried from high school. Todd wanted her brokenness, her mess, and her insecurities. He reaffirmed the qualities he saw in her that she couldn't always see herself. Todd wanted her joy and her generosity and her encouragement. He wanted her heart. So why was she holding back?

Unsure of why the doubts still circled, she sent a wordless cry heavenward. Suddenly, the anxiety and insecurity vanished and the complete certainty of her answer filled her. She looked back at Todd, who was still studying her face with ring in hand, a look of vulnerability on his face.

"Yes! I say yes!" The answer burst from her lips with a smile.

"You do?" Todd seemed surprised.

"Yes! I don't know what was holding me back, but honestly, there is nothing I want more than to partner with you. For eternity. It's scary to be offered everything I've dreamed of. It seems too good to be true, but I know it is."

Chrissy looked into his eyes and saw her future in them. "I know you and I don't need months of dating to discover what we already know. Todd, I love you so much. I think that's why it hurt so much to find out about your lies. I loved you even then, before I had admitted to myself. So, I'm saying yes. Let's do this." She launched herself into his arms and lifted her head for the kisses she desperately wanted.

Todd was only too happy to oblige. He wrapped her in his strong arms and covered her mouth with his. When they parted, he took the ring from its small black velvet box and removed her left hand from where it rested on his chest, gently placing the ring on her ring finger. "There. I've been wishing for this moment for years. And my wish finally came true."

AFTER DINNER AND A HALLMARK MOVIE, Todd convinced Chrissy they should take the sign to the cafe to hang it up. The renovations would start very soon, and while Todd would schedule the project so that the restaurant could be open as much as possible, it would have to close for a few weeks. Announcing to the community the reopening of the bistro would need to happen soon.

When they arrived at the cafe, Chrissy opened the back door and Todd followed her holding the sign. As tey walked through the kitchen and the smell of warm food immediately hit Chrissy.

Abruptly, her family and friends jumped up from behind the counter with a loud shout. "Surprise!"

With a wide smile, she passed from the kitchen into the front of the restaurant. Food was laid out on several trays sitting on the counter, along with New Year's hats and noisemakers. Plastic champagne flutes, bottles of sparkling grape juice, and champagne sat at one of the tables. A wrinkled banner hung from the ceiling that read "Congratulations!" and another read "Happy New Year!"

Chrissy looked back at Todd and saw his guilty smile. Chrissy was thrilled to see her parents and immediately went to give them a hug. Mandy, Luke, Charlotte and several other close friends rounded out the group. Charlotte immediately zeroed in on the ring prominently displayed on Chrissy's left hand.

"Ahh, Congratulations!" Charlotte said as she grabbed Chrissy's hand to inspect the ring further.

Todd overheard the exchange and started to wave his arms to quiet everyone so he could speak. He put an arm around Chrissy and spoke to the group, "Thank you all so much for coming. I was hoping we would have a lot to celebrate here tonight. First of all—I couldn't be happier that Chrissy has agreed to put up with me for the rest of our lives!" Applause broke out among the small group of friends. Chrissy tucked an embarrassed smile toward Todd's strong frame. After the applause died down, Todd continued. "And secondly, Chrissy has an announcement about Bud and Janine's Cafe." He gestured for her to take over.

With a small nod, she stepped out of his embrace and took a deep breath. She didn't really care for being the center of attention, but these were her friends and this was her business.

Speaking first to her parents, she started. "Mom and Dad, Bud and Janine's has been part of the landscape of Minden for decades. It is a place where friends meet, families break bread, and community thrives. And I want nothing more than for that legacy to continue for the next fifty years." Her focus shifted away from her parents. "That's why the cafe will be closing periodically over the next two months to allow my very talented fiancé," she blushed at the word, " to do some much-needed renovation. With our extraordinary new chef, Norm, and a newly renovated space, Bud and Janine's Cafe will be reopening as B&Js Bistro with an updated menu and new feel." Todd held up the bistro sign for everyone to see and was rewarded with the hum of murmured approval.

"Our goals will always be delicious food at affordable prices and a place where community and friendship are the center of everything. We," she gestured to herself and Todd, "cannot wait to show you what we have planned. Our grand reopening is scheduled for Valentine's Day, and you all better be there!" Everyone laughed at her mock serious tone.

"Well, it looks like Norm made some delicious food for us to enjoy tonight, perhaps a sneak peek of dishes that will grace the menu of the new bistro. If you've eaten here in the last couple of weeks, you already know how amazing his cooking is. I'm so excited for you to experience the heights of flavor that he will achieve when I let him loose in the kitchen with his creativity and skill." Todd started clapping and the others joined in as she finished, "Seriously, thank you all so much for coming tonight and celebrating with us. You are the best."

The rest of the evening was spent enjoying the company of her friends and family. Her mother and father both spoke their approval of Todd and their excitement about the changes to the restaurant. Norm's appetizer trays were delicious. Despite the spaghetti they'd had at Todd's house earlier, she couldn't help having a second small plate of the spinach artichoke dip, maple-glazed bacon-wrapped water chestnuts, and buffalo chicken bites. She fielded all sorts of questions she hadn't even begun to consider about the wedding, like if they had picked a date or what colors and flowers she would choose. When she got a second alone with Todd, she mentioned the questions to him. "I definitely want to wait until after the bistro reopens before we do anything," she said as though it were a foregone conclusion.

Todd looked slightly disappointed. "More than two months?" He took a deep breath and then smiled at her lovingly. "I've waited twenty years to make you mine, Chris. I'm sure I can make it another couple of months." When midnight rolled around, the group counted down loudly and Chrissy looked deep in Todd's eyes with each number. The noise of the party faded into the background.

Five. Four. *I love this man.* Three. *Next year is going to be the best year ever.* Two. *We are getting married!* One. *Oh, now I get to kiss him, right?* Applause and noisemakers filled the small space, but she barely heard it. "Happy New Year," she whispered as he captured her mouth with his.

EPILOGUE

*M*andy cringed at her reflection and removed the T-shirt, stained from where Miles spit up on her earlier. The precious infant was a joy to snuggle, but she was always ready to hand him back to his parents.

Other than the exchange of candy and Valentine's cards with her daycare kids, Mandy had hoped to ignore Valentine's Day this year. Single Awareness Day, she'd heard someone call it, which was far too accurate. Plus, she couldn't mope in her living room with a Hallmark movie tonight; it was Chrissy's grand re-opening. What kind of friend would she be if she didn't go?

Twenty minutes later, Mandy stepped into the restaurant, taking in the changes. It was like an entirely new place with a cozy, chic vibe that made her smile. Chrissy had been gushing about all the changes for months, but seeing it in person was something special. The lights were dimmed, giving the entire restaurant a romantic feel. Luke and Charlotte sat sipping from coffee mugs, cuddled on the new couch near the front window. *Newlyweds.* Mandy felt the twinge of jealousy. A year ago, she thought Luke was the one for her, but she had to admit he and Charlotte were perfect together.

Mandy made her way to the counter and gave Chrissy a hug. Her friend was positively glowing, all dressed up in a flattering wrap dress of deep red. While Mandy stood, studying the appetizers laid out on the counter, Todd came through the kitchen and caught sight of Chrissy. "Wow. You look... stunning."

Chrissy blushed. "You don't think it is too much for Minden?" Todd shook his head, and she turned to Mandy. "What do you think?"

"You look beautiful, Chrissy. And so does this place. Great job, Todd."

Todd pulled Chrissy close with an arm. "I'm just the muscle. She's the brains." Chrissy blushed and he kissed the top of her head.

Mandy watched their sweet exchange with a frozen smile. Would it ever get easier to see people happy and in love? Chrissy's mom joined the conversation, "You look great, Christine."

Chrissy looked up at her mom with a question in her eyes.

"You do. You look happy and successful and that dress fits you wonderfully. I mean, clearly you need a haircut, but the style you chose disguises that fact pretty well." Mandy couldn't help but think her own mother would say something similar.

"I think her hair looks great." Todd spoke up as he twirled a curl around his finger and gave Chrissy a look filled with love.

Unwilling to listen to the lovebirds any longer, Mandy made her excuses and fixed herself a plate. Mandy had worked at the cafe enough to know Norm was a genius in the kitchen. As she added another mini sandwich to her plate, he stepped out of the kitchen and began refilling the trays.

"She's done good, hasn't she?" Norm spoke with unexpected emotion, gesturing to Chrissy across the room with his tongs.

Mandy smiled, looking at her friend with pride. "Yeah, she has. This bistro is going to be exactly what Minden needs." She didn't begrudge her friend's happiness. Chrissy had worked hard for the restaurant, and it was frankly about time she and Todd had figured out the obvious.

At 8:00, Chrissy and Todd each said a few words to thank everyone for coming, encouraging them to leave reviews online, and to solicit applause for Norm, who was able to duck out of the kitchen only briefly throughout the night.

After their speech, Mandy headed for the door, looking forward to her flannel pajamas and the ice cream in her freezer, she caught up with Todd and Chrissy one last time, stopping just shy of their table as Todd pulled a small, beautifully wrapped present out of his pocket and gave it to Chrissy. "Now it's time to plan that wedding. And that honeymoon."

Chrissy shook her head. "You shouldn't have gotten me anything!"

Mandy saw a leather passport cover, embroidered with the initials C.E.F and saw Todd whisper something in Chrissy's ear. Chrissy opened the thin billfold-like case and saw two airplane tickets. Her mouth fell open and she gasped. "Italy?!"

Todd grinned. "Yep. I figure we've been to Eataly and now we should see the real thing. I want to see the world with you, Chris. I don't ever want you to let fear hold you back again."

Instead of interrupting, Mandy bit her lip and turned toward the exit. Chrissy deserved to enjoy every minute of today, and Mandy would rather escape from this romantic atmosphere and all the happy couples surrounding her. She would see Chrissy tomorrow, when her own pity party wouldn't ruin the moment.

WILL MANDY FIND TRUE LOVE? Read Spring Fever, the next book in the Main Street Minden Series now!

NOTE TO READERS

To my readers - thank you for picking up (or downloading!) this book. I am an avid reader and can never have to many books on my bookshelf or in my ereader. As any author can tell you, reviews are incredibly important to our success. Please please please take a minute to leave a review. Also, you can learn more about my upcoming projects at my website: www.taragraceericson.com or by signing up for my newsletter. Follow me on Facebook for chances to win advanced reader copies, see sneak peeks of upcoming books, and my book recommendations or random thoughts!

As much as I love a good Amish or "Old West" romance novel filled with stories of love and faith and family; I became frustrated that so much of the

Christian Romance genre was dominated with stories of another time period—as though it is impossible to live out your faith in the world of today, or find romance without going back in time. So I started writing my own. I hope you enjoyed it and that it was a worthwhile use of your time. I pray it encouraged you in your faith and your struggles. I look forward to sharing the stories of many more characters with you - especially the ones in Minden.

ACKNOWLEDGMENTS

Above all, to my Abba Father - without you, the rest of this is nothing. You've blessed me with so much. May my words and deeds be a blessing to You.

Thank you to my friends and family, without whose support and encouragement, I would have given up a long time ago. Especially, to my husband - you are my rock and I love doing life with you. This adventure continues to be one I wouldn't trade for any other. As we welcome the newest addition to our little family, I can't help but to be thankful for the wonderful father, husband, and man that you are. To Mr. B - for the endless hugs and laughter and songs. I love you more than you will ever understand.

Special thanks to Gabbi, who lets me bounce ideas off of her and doesn't mind when I spoil the ending or send her the kissing scenes to enjoy ahead of time! And to my mother - the editor. Your support and encouragement have brought me here, along with your ability to spot an errant comma or extra word.

To Jessica, my lovely first reader turned editor. Your insight and constructive feedback is spot on, every time! I am so grateful we are friends. You make me a better person, writer, and mother.

To all the readers of my first book who messaged me telling me how much you were enjoying it. Those notes kept me going when I needed the extra motivation!

Lastly, to the team at my local Starbucks - for the caffeine, the laughter, and the WiFi.

ABOUT THE AUTHOR

Tara Grace Ericson lives in Missouri with her husband and two sons. She studied engineering and worked as an engineer for many years before embracing her creative side to become a full-time author.

Her first book, Falling on Main Street, was written mostly from airport waiting areas and bleak hotel rooms as she traveled in her position as a sales engineer. She loves cooking, crocheting, and reading books by the dozen.

Her writing partner is usually her black lab - Ruby - and a good cup of coffee or tea. Tara unashamedly watches Hallmark movies all winter long, even though they are predictable and cheesy.

She loves a good "happily ever after" with an engaging love story. That's why Tara focuses on writing clean contemporary romance, with an emphasis on Christian faith and living. She wants to encourage her readers with stories of men and women who live out their faith in tough situations.

BOOKS BY TARA GRACE ERICSON

The Main Street Minden Series

Falling on Main Street

Winter Wishes

Spring Fever

Summer to Remember

Kissing in the Kitchen: A Main Street Minden Novella

The Bloom Sisters Series

Hoping for Hawthorne: A Bloom Family Novella

A Date For Daisy

Poppy's Proposal